Contents

For

JAN VAN BEERS

Chapter 1

Black Magic in the Wood

THERE came to Deep Wood, one summer's night, a strange and mysterious Happening. The Wood lies to the west of the Wild River, on the eastern bank of which Sweethallow Valley slopes downwards to its green and secret depths. This queer Happening came in many small ways and at many different times—now it would appear in Badger's Beech where Old Stripe lives his quiet days; then it would be seen on Otter's Island, where Potter-the-Otter spends his time making quaint pottery on his ancient wheel; and sometimes it would be heard—or felt—in Woo's Glade, where stands Owl's Beech, one of the most stately timbers in all the land.

In so many ways and forms and sounds and shapes did this strange Black Magic come to the Wood, that perhaps it would be better to start at the beginning, and tell the tale of it in all its parts until the end of it.

The end of the story is a very long way from the beginning; and many puzzling things lie in the middle.

7

Black Magic in the Wood

It all began, then, this Summer's night when Old Stripe, the Badger of Badger's Beech, was sitting quietly by his doorstep, a-smoking of his last pipe of the day. It was twilight, and the skies were deep blue velvet above the dreaming trees. A myriad stars were spread like a cloth of bright sequins, glinting and gleaming beyond the dark-green tracery of the leaves. The air was still with that breathless calm that comes to a Summer night, when there is no breeze among the trees, and no voice to break the stillness save for the quiet piping of a distant bird, or the soft footsteps of some folk late on his way home to a burrow or a dwelling deep beneath the leaves.

Old Stripe blinked slowly about him, thinking what a pleasant and a friendly place this Woodland surely was; and as he blinked he gave a sigh of deep contentment; and as he sighed, a little blue plume of smoke went a-drifting upwards in the quiet air, scenting it with the sweet smell of clover and of coltsfoot, that he used for the blending of his favourite tobacco.

As the twilight deepened into gloom, and shadows were sprawling everywhere among the tree-boles, Stripe got to his feet and struck a tinder to light his candle-lantern that hung above his front door. He would be off to bed before long, as soon as he'd smoked the last sweet strand of his tobacco; but a folk never knew when another folk might chance to happen along to call on him, by way of 'How-are-you' or 'Good-night' or 'Well-I-*am*-Surprised!' And it was a pleasant thing to be going to bed with—the echo of a friendly voice before the night came down.

So the Badger lit his lantern, and closed the little glass door of it, watching the bright and shining flame as it leaped inside, to cast a pale glow upon the tree, and to chase the shadows from the shallow flight of steps.

'Heigh-ho . . . ' murmured the black-and-white-striped folk, and sat down on his old kitchen chair to smoke the last of his evening pipe. For a moment he went on blinking contentedly about him, wondering if some-folk might happen along for a chat, and wondering whom it might be if one did; then he blinked less contentedly and much more quickly into the gloom. In fact he looked most and exceptional surprised, of a sudden.

A moment ago there had been the pale sheen of lantern-light, shining from the candle above him. Now it was gone and nothing but deep shadow remained.

'Tch-tch-tch!' he said severely, and frowned up at his lantern in puzzlement. 'Now *there's* a funny thing to go and happen on a Summer's night!'

He took his tinder-box, opened the door of the lamp, and lit the wick again. It leaped up, bright as ever.

9

'I should think so, too . . . ' Stripe nodded firmly, and returned to his chair, wondering what had made his candle go out—for there was no breeze here, and in any case his lantern had been known to burn brightly through many a Winter gale, to show folk where there was a bit of warmth and welcome on their way through the Wood.

'Funny things,' he murmured to himself, closing his eyes dreamily and testing the full rich flavour of his tobacco, 'candles are. Never can tell what they're going to get up to next, that's the trouble with candles.'

He didn't know just how right his words were going to prove, for when he opened his eyes to see how the night was a-getting on, it was pale and starlit, with not a single gleam from his lantern above the steps.

'I'm dreaming,' he said to himself, and closed his eyes again to make sure. Then he opened one of them, very slowly and cautiously, and peered in puzzlement at the lamp. It was out, and cold, and dark. So he opened his other eye, just as slowly and as cautiously, and looked at the lantern with that one too. But it was still out, and cold, and dark.

'This,' declared Old Stripe in amazement and annoyance, 'requires looking-into!' And he got up and opened the door of the lamp, peering inside. The candle stood there, doing nothing at all except stand and look candly; and the wick was very black and smelt of cold candle-wick, nothing more.

Black Magic in the Wood

'It is quite obvimous,' said the Badger (who sometimes got his words a little mixed and confused), 'that something is the matter here.' And he blinked deedily at his candle while he wondered what it could possibly be. When he'd finished wondering, he decided that he just couldn't think, so he tried once more before he took serious action. Lighting the wick again, he waited until the flame was bright and clear as a yellow crocus; then he blew into the lantern. Sure enough, the flame flickered and danced about in sudden surprise—but it didn't go out. When Stripe stopped blowing, the flame stood straight and shining again, throwing a goodly light all around the steps and the front door and that portion of the tree-trunk that was handy.

'Then it wasn't the breeze,' said Stripe, closing the lantern door. 'And there wasn't a breeze anyway, so it couldn't have been, twice.'

Thinking deeply about the curious ways of his lamp—which had served him well for many a year, just as it had his father—he stood quite still on the top step and stared stonily at it, almost as though he were daring it to go out again. He stared at it so long and stonily that his eyes began aching, so he stopped. The candle burned steadily on, as though it had been well behaved all the evening.

Old Stripe gave a slow nod and a satisfied sigh, and was just going to take the kitchen chair into the house—since it wasn't very likely anyfolk would be wanting to sit on it out here during the night—when he stopped. Because it was suddenly dark again.

After a long gloomy silence, while he thought much about Candles and Lanterns and the Curious and Peculiar Way in which they seemed to Carry On, he said firmly:

'This—is—*too*—much.' (Because it surely was.) Then he added, to make sure: 'this is very *much* too much.' After declaring this in a loud and annoyed tone, to prove to himself just how annoyed he felt about things in general and out-going candles in particular, he put his kitchen chair in the hall, closed his front door, climbed the shallow flight of steps leading to the mossy pathway outside the beech-tree, and went stomping off through the Wood, for as he said to himself—and to anyfolk who happened to overhear him—

'I must go and see old Potter about this, I don't care *how* late it is!'

He left the glade and entered the thickly-clustered coppice on the way to the Wild River. 'There's not a breath of a breeze,' he muttered as he walked, 'so the candle wasn't blown out.'

He neared the River, and heard the first faint murmur of it as it ran and tumbled under the starry heavens. 'And no-folk came along and pinched the wick,' he added thoughtfully, 'so it wasn't that.'

Leaving the trees, he went along the brown pathway that led to the little mooring-place where

Potter kept his rowing boat, *Bunty*. 'And I don't see any other reason a candle can possimously have,' he decided firmly, 'for going out when it's been lit all proper and according to the best rules about candle-lighting. So it went out without any reason at all.'

He reached the mooring-post, and saw the little blue boat that was left there by the Otter for those of his friends who couldn't swim or didn't particularly want to.

'Good,' he nodded, and climbed on board, taking up the oars after casting the rope free. 'Now we shall see what old Potter has to say about things.'

* * *

Potter-the-Otter was sitting outside his house on Otter's Island, with a tankard of sweet cherry-ale held comfortably in his furry old paw, watching his River flowing by. Above the trees, the stars were still and gleaming silently; but in the water they danced and jigged to the music of the ripples, as though a thousand tiny boats were drifting there, each with a lantern of bright silver at the mast.

The sound of the River was friendly to the ears of this water-folk; for this was his island, where his ancestors had dwelled in days past. So long had the Otters lived on the Wild River that they had come to look upon it as their own; and, in a way, it was. There was another sound that Potter listened to as he sat dreaming this Summer's night, and it was made by the little water-wheel that turned his potter's clay for him in the workshop deep in the house. The voice of it was a joy in his ears as the stout vanes went turning to the current, sending up beads of water that scattered like pearls in the starlight before they dropped, sowing a skein of jewels to the ripples' furrowed way.

In normal times the wheel would not be turning, unless Potter were turning at his clay; but this evening he had forgotten to throw the lever that held the vanes, and now they turned on, sending water-music to the breathless air.

'It's a very bad thing,' muttered the Otter, as he sat a-sipping of his ale. 'Leaving my water-wheel going. It wears the shafts and the cogs, that's what it does. So I'll go and attend to it.'

He made no effort to move from the log on which he sat. So long as he told himself it was a Bad Thing, it eased his conscience until he gathered the energy to go and see to it.

'A very bad thing indeed,' he nodded sadly, and sipped at his tankard again. He'd been telling himself how bad a thing it was, ever since he had come out here to sit the evening through; and now that the night was almost here he had the feeling that it was really high time to prove his words.

Very carefully, so as not to surprise his legs too much and make them tottery, he stood up and gave a deep sigh that was a mixture of contentment and sadness. He felt most and extreme contented with the evening and the peace of it and his tankard of cherry-ale; but there was a sadness because now he had to go into the house to stop the water-wheel. That required not only some stuff called Energy (of which he possessed very little); but also that the delicious sound of the vanes churning through the water must cease.

He was just opening the front door, meaning to pass through the hall and the sitting-room and the kitchen and the scullery until he reached his pottering-room, when he stopped, his paw still on the door-knob. It wasn't a very surprising sort of knob; and the door was quite an ordinary kind made of wood and wrought-iron hinges and decorations; so it was neither of them that made him pause. No, he was suddenly aware that something was *missing*.

With his furry old head on one side, he stood there in the stillness and listened to all the river-sounds—except one.

'Well, bless me whiskers!' he murmured in puzzlement.

The voice of the water-wheel had stopped, and only the ripples ran on, gurgling under the night-sky.

Potter, who was a true river-folk, knew what a serious thing it was when a water-wheel stopped of its own accord; for it usually meant that something like a spar of drift-wood or a length of fallen bough had jammed in the vanes. And *that* meant the vanes were in danger of being broken if the current were strong enough.

Potter-the-Otter put down his ale-tankard and trotted briskly round the corner of the snug little house and looked at his water-wheel. There it was, with the vanes reflecting the silent starfields on their wet-shining surface; but the wheel was still as stone.

There was a splash as the Otter dived straight into the ripples, holding his breath as he went down, down, into the cool depths until he felt the round smoothness of the pebbles on the river-bed. Though he could see very little, deep here under the surface where no starglow was, he knew his wheel as though it were part of him. His paws felt the vanes and the spindle all over; yet there was no drift-wood nor any loose bough or branch caught in the wheel.

The ripples burst into silver spray as he shot to the surface and took a deep breath of air. Within a moment he was climbing the sandy bank and shaking the water from his fur. All through the hall and the kitchen and the scullery were small dark footprints as he hastened into the pottery-room. But there was nothing to stop the potter's-wheel turning, and nothing obstructing the shafts that ran through the wall to the water-mill.

'If this isn't the peculiarmost thing as ever happened to anything in all of a folk's days,' he

declared to the candle he was holding, 'then I don't
know what is. Or was. Or something.' And he tried
to think what is, or was, or something, while he was
also trying to think why his wheel had stopped.

After he'd gazed at the shafts and cogs in the
candle-light for a long time, and still couldn't make

it out, he left the house again and looked at the
wheel. The ripples ran chuckling past the unmoving
vanes, as though they knew the secret of this
curious puzzle.

Watching his wheel in the stillness, trying to think
what could be amiss, Potter-the-Otter was startled
by the sudden sound of it as suddenly the vanes

went spinning and the wheel went churning and the water went splashing and tumbling over itself to leap and dance in the starlight as though all the lamps in the heavens were clustered here for making-merry of a sudden.

Potter blinked in surprise. Things were getting better—and at the same time, worse. He was happy to see his water-wheel frolicking round again; but there was still a double puzzle: why had it stopped, when there'd been no reason? And why was it going again, without his touching it?

He stayed by the riverside for so long, trying to answer all the questions his furry old mind was asking of itself, that he felt quite tired, and turned for his front-door again.

His hand was on the knob, just as it had been before, when the very same thing happened. A hush had come to the river; and the voice of the wheel was silent.

Something chilly seemed to trickle all the way down the Otter's spine, and when this icy trickle reached the tip of his tail, he gave a shiver and turned back to look at the wheel.

Now Potter was a brave folk, as bold as any in the Wood; and he threw off the creepy, ghosty feeling that was on him, and dived into the water. Again he felt for obstructions; and again he went into the pottery-room to make sure there was nothing in the way of the shafts. Again there was no answer to

18

the mystery. For when he went out of the house for the last time, he heard the sudden rushing of the waters and saw the sudden leaping of the sparkling spray and knew that somehow it had begun turning again, as though an invisible folk were playing tricks on him.

Even the brave-and-bold Potter could stand this sort of thing no longer. There was something very queer a-going on in the Wild River, and he felt the need to talk it over with somefolk, to see if they might have a suggestion to make. In any case he didn't feel inclined to go to bed while such mysterious happenings were disturbing the night.

He was turning the corner of his house and making for the other bank of the Island, intending to swim across, when he heard a new sound: that of water slapping against the beams of a boat, and the slow plying of oars. When he lifted his head and gazed across the pale-lit waters, he saw the dark shape of little *Bunty*, nearing the Island.

'Hello there!' he called, wondering whom it might be a-visiting him so late at night.

For a moment the oars ceased, and a voice came back like an echo:

'Hello there, Potter—is that you?'

'I don't know,' called the Otter, still confused with all these mysteries. 'I—I mean of course it's me. Who are you?'

19

But he saw who his visitor was, as soon as the Badger stopped 'rowing and let *Bunty* glide into her mooring-creek on the shore of the Island.

Potter lent him a helping paw, and cast the looped rope round a mooring-post.

'I'm glad you came, Old Stripe. I was just coming over to Badger's Beech, funnily enough.'

'Were you indeed?' said Stripe, a puzzled frown still on his brow. 'Well, there are funnier things than that a-going on tonight, and I've come to ask you what you think of them.'

Potter-the-Otter looked at his good friend in the half-light, wondering if Stripe had been having queer things going on at his Beech, just as there were on the Island.

'Well, let's go into the house,' he suggested quietly, 'and talk about it over a pot of coffee, shall we?'

Old Stripe nodded, and offered his tobacco-pouch to the Otter as they turned from the shore. Potter filled his cherrywood pipe slowly and carefully, thinking how strange and mysterious a night it had become; then he struck a tinder-flame and lit the golden strands of clover in the bowl; and then, just as he opened the front door, he heard it again— that sudden hush over the waters, as the voice of the water-wheel was stilled.

'Old Stripe,' he breathed softly as they went into the hall, 'there's magic in the trees tonight.'

Black Magic in the Wood

'Black magic,' nodded his friend, wondering how Potter could know. He followed his host into the kitchen, where a kettle was already singing a ditty on the hob.

Chapter 2

The Meeting at Owl's Beech

THE folk of the Wood were troubled.

From Fallen Elm came little Skip Squirrel, with the story of how his milk had turned sour on three different occasions; yet there was no thunder, nor any other reason. Every new morning he had gone to the meadows and collected his cowslip-milk; and every noon it was sour. He must see a folk about it, so he went from Fallen Elm along the path by the Wild River and turned to the West through the glades until he came to Badger's Beech. Old Stripe would know.

The folk of Deep Wood were troubled.

From Fox End came another one, hurrying through the trees. Three times had Scruff Fox lighted his bonfire behind the marrow-beds, and three times it had gone out. He had coaxed and cajoled the heap of rubbish to burn, for it was as dry as tinder. He had even taken a candle from his woodshed and tinder from his box, and set them flaring below the pile of bone-dry refuse—and still there was no flame from it. Scruff Fox had been lighting his bonfires every spring and every autumn for more years then he could count on all the bristles of his garden-broom, and now he was having bother. So he made through the copses for Badger's Beech, his furry old brow as wrinkled as a walnut. Old Stripe would tell him what was wrong.

The folk of the Wood were troubled.

From the little shop that nestled below the eaves of Silver-Birch Hill came old Mr. Nibble the Rabbit, his tall brown ears a-going flop-flop-flop as his hurrying feet took him urgently for the Badger's glade. Every morning it was the same—he'd arrange all his wares in their separate boxes and stay in the shop the day long: yet when evening came there was nothing but a higgledy-piggledy confusion—nuts in the tobacco-jars; herbs among the honey; candles in the jam-pots and parchment on the floor. There was a folk at mischief somewhere, and he wondered who. Old Stripe would know.

The folk of the Wood were troubled. From spinney and copse, from the high nests among the elm trees, from burrow and from bush they came worrying and hurrying to ask the Badger what he thought of things.

Old Stripe opened his door to them, three days after his own candle-lantern had thrown such curious fits when he'd been smoking of his pipe while the twilight shone.

'I'm getting tired of it!' declared Skip Squirrel, as he helped the Badger to make more dandelion-tea for all his visitors.

'It wants looking into,' nodded Scruff Fox, passing round the cups and the saucers and the spoons. 'I've made my bonfires forty years and more, just as my grand-Fox did before me, and all I can say is—'

'Something must be done!' declared Potter-the-Otter, whose water-wheel had never been right since three nights ago, when the Badger had come to see him on the Island.

'Well I'm sure *I* don't know what's about,' said Stripe, 'for I'm just as bothered as you folk. My pipe tastes funny no matter what I do with my tobacco; and twice I've dropped a basin in the kitchen and broken it; and only yesterday I lit my fire and all the smoke went billowing into the pantry before I could turn round. And that's apart from the way my candle behaves over the front door.'

They talked it over, the Badgers and Otters and Squirrels and Stoats and Hares, while Old Stripe scratched the tips of his ears to help him think, and Potter pulled reflectively at his fine long tail, and Mole-the-Miller from Heather Hill stroked his smooth black velvety chest and shook his head.

'It's the most puzzly thing I've heard of in all me time,' he said, 'and I can only think it's the Tall Timberfolk playing their tricks.'

Everyone was silent, and they looked at Mole.

'The folk of Tall Timberland?' murmured Scruff Fox. He lifted his head and blinked deedily at Old Stripe's ceiling, wondering if it were they. 'What would they want to play tricks on us for?'

'You know *them*,' said Skip Squirrel, 'always looking for something new to keep them busy.'

'But they're quite ordinary folk,' protested Potter.

'They couldn't make Old Stripe's candle go out, or my water-wheel stop turning—'

'Or my milk turn sour,' Skip shook his little brown head, 'or Mr. Nibble's shop all of a pickle.'

'It can't be the Tall Timberfolk,' agreed Mole-the-Miller, 'but it just occurred to me.'

It was evening before folk began going off to their homes; but no one had thought of anything to explain the mysterious happenings in the Wood. It was when Stripe was standing at his front door with Potter and Skip Squirrel, saying good-night to his visitors, that Scruff Fox said suddenly:

'That's funny.'

'What is?' asked Skip, hoping some new kind of trickery wasn't beginning of a sudden.

'Woo Owl,' said Scruff, frowning over his pipe.

'What about Woo Owl?' asked Potter.

'He isn't here,' explained the Fox, thinking things out very carefully in his slow and serious way.

'That's right,' said Skip. 'He lives in Owl's Beech, that's why he isn't here.'

'Everyone else,' said Scruff slowly, 'lives everywhere else, but *they're* all here, or have been.'

Skip Squirrel looked in alarm at Old Stripe, who was frowning deeply at Potter-the-Otter. Potter-the-Otter gave a jump of uneasiness and put their thoughts into words:

'Has anything queer been happening to *him?*'

26

'Don't know,' said Stripe, 'but we must go and see, at once!'

'Before it does!' nodded Skip.

'If it hasn't already,' said Scruff Fox gloomily.

Old Stripe trotted briskly down to the kitchen to see that the kettle wasn't left on the hob and that all the windows were closed; then he joined his three friends at the steps and went with them along the pathway to Woo's Glade, where the giant beech tree stood.

'There's no smoke going up from the chimneys,' said Skip Squirrel, as they looked up at the mighty timber.

'It's Summer-time,' grunted Scruff.

'His front door isn't open,' persisted Skip, quite convinced that something had happened to their friend the Owl.

'Then he must be out,' said Stripe.

'Or in,' said Potter, 'and not wanting a draught from the front doorway.'

'We'll soon find out,' Stripe told them. 'Up you go, Skip Squirrel!'

The small brown folk went up the ladder that was put there by Owl for his visitors who couldn't fly or didn't particularly want to when they were visiting him; and Old Stripe and Potter and Scruff Fox followed, until they stood in a serious group on Woo's front porch.

'Give a knock,' suggested Scruff, still wondering

27

with part of his furry old mind about his bonfires, and why they wouldn't burn.

'Just a small knock, said Skip, thinking about his milk and the way it had turned sour, 'not to startle him.'

'There's my water-wheel going again,' said Potter, his head on one side as he listened to the Wild River as it ran past the Island, not far away. 'And I stopped it before I came out this morning, too!'

While he was listening to the rushing of the water-wheel and Scruff was thinking of bonfires and Skip was wondering about his milk, Old Stripe lifted the ancient knocker on Woo Owl's front door and let it fall.

'Don't believe he's in,' said Skip after a moment.

'Give him time, he might be cooking his supper.'

'I think something's happened to him.'

'Then we'll help him with it, whatever it is.'

'Give him another knock.'

But just as Stripe raised his paw to the knocker, the door opened quickly and he knocked on a small polished beak that was suddenly there.

'Have a care!' suggested Woo Owl mildly, as Stripe stopped knocking on his nose.

'Beg pardon, I'm sure,' said the Badger. 'You opened the door too quickly. Are you all right?'

'All right?' Woo asked, blinking largely at this sudden assembly on his front porch.

'Has anything happened?' asked Skip.

The Meeting at Owl's Beech

'Happened?' Woo Owl regarded his visitors with his big wings folded behind his large feathery back. 'What sort of happen do you mean?'

They looked at him in puzzlement. Certainly their good friend-with-the-feathers *looked* all right and seemed as healthy and as untroubled as ever; but they found it hard to believe that only he out of all the Woodlanders had been left in peace by whatever Goblin or Will-o'-the-Wisp was at work in the trees.

'Isn't your milk sour?' enquired little Skip Squirrel kindly. Woo Owl regarded him with a lofty frown.

'My milk,' he said heavily, 'is most certainly *not* sour, my dear Skip Squirrel.'

'Isn't your water-wheel playing tricks?' asked Potter, without thinking.

'To my knowledge,' replied Woo Owl, 'there is *no* water-wheel in Owl's Beech.' He looked very hard at Potter-the-Otter, wondering perhaps if he were dozing on his feet. 'Unless of course somebody has built one in my bath-tub,' he concluded with mild sarcasm.

'And how's your bonfire?' enquired Scruff Fox with genuine interest. It was useless for Owl to protest that he had no bonfire, because every self-respecting folk had one of those. It seemed, however, that Woo Owl was not aware of this.

'Bonfire?' he asked, scandalized. And he blinked

very largely at Scruff Fox. He was beginning to wonder, indeed, if these folk hadn't been holding some sort of feast, where the wine had perhaps flowed freely . . . 'I suppose you folk haven't been drinking applejack, have you?' he asked outright.

Old Stripe scratched his head and then shook it slowly; he was really becoming a little confused with all these queer happenings a-going on in the Wood; and there'd been so much discussion about them all day long that he was beginning to think it might all be a sort of nightmare.

'I don't *think* we've been drinking anything of *that* sort,' he said simply. And he rolled his tongue round and round to see if there were anything applejacky left to taste.

'Then you'd better come inside,' said Woo Owl, 'and then we'll see what everything seems to be about.'

'Good,' nodded Potter. 'I think we ought to hold another meeting, over a pot of coffee or tea or—'

'Potter,' Old Stripe interrupted him, 'remember we are about to be guests here.'

'Er—oh, exactly, Old Stripe. I just meant—'

'My dear Potter,' said Owl largely, 'I shouldn't dream of entertaining you without such niceties as you mention. Now come along in, and we'll settle down on my veranda at the top of the tree.'

One by one the puzzled and bewildered folk

followed their host into the tree, and Skip Squirrel closed the door. They went through the wide hallway into the sitting-room, up the stairs that ran round the wall of the big circular room and into the sun-parlour, up the next flight of stairs to the middle landing, and on and on and up and up until they came to the lofty loggia at the very top of the tree. From here there opened two long doors leading onto the veranda that Woo had built with the help of his friends.

'Every time I come out here,' said Old Stripe with a comfortable sigh, 'I think the view looks more wonderful.'

They gazed around them in the twilight. Just over their heads, the leaves moved gently to an errant breeze that crept from Heather Hill and touched the ripples of the Wild River before it was lost in the secret spinneys beyond the deep green banks. From here a folk could see much of the Wood—Silver-Birch Hill, and the quaint red roof of Mr. Nibble's shop; the ancient mill above the heathered slopes, where the Mole made snow-white flour for his friends and neighbours; and Otter's Island, a small green haven set in the river's blue like emerald on sapphire in the quiet evening light.

From here a folk could see even the depths of Sweethallow Valley, where lived the Chipmunks and the Gray Squirrels; and the narrow stream that meandered at the foot of the pine-clad slopes. Just now, when the last of the sunset was threaded as spun-gold among the lacy clouds to the West, the Valley was most beautiful. A slow mist was rising from the stream and about the meadows, and the lamps and the lanterns of the Valley-folk shone as small stars through the twilight's hue. The pines and the cedars reared, ranged in shadow, as though they stood upon the slopes to dream until the sun came again to deck them in their own bright green.

'There's wind coming,' murmured Potter, his voice breaking the stillness here. The Otter knew all about wind, just as he knew the moods of his river. By the way the ripples shifted, or grew in size or lessened, he knew many things of the weather, especially the wind.

'Then we'll hold our meeting in the sun-parlour,' Woo Owl suggested, 'so we can watch the wind when it gets up.'

The sun-parlour, a round room like all the Owl's rooms in this majestic beech, had windows that looked out to all points of the compass; and to the East there were long, deep windows from which a folk could see half Sweethallow and most of the Wild River where it followed the boundary of the Wood.

'Now tell me all about these absurd occurrences,' said Woo, when he had settled his friends with cushions and chairs and cups of coffee and plates of nutmeg cake and walnut scones.

The Meeting at Owl's Beech

At first he understood not one word, for they began talking at once. All he could pick out of the general confusion was an occasional 'bonfire' and sometimes 'water-wheel' and now and then the mention of 'sour milk.' At last he quietened them down and made them tell him their story one by one. After having heard which, he said simply:

'Of course it's just a lot of nonsense!'

Old Stripe stopped sipping his coffee and looked at Woo Owl very seriously.

'I don't think it's nonsense at all, my dear Woo. I'm very glad nothing has come along to disturb you; but if it had, then you'd know what we mean. What about my candle, for instance, above the front door?'

'Simple,' declared Woo, blinking largely from a huge armchair near the south window. 'It was a draught, of course.'

'There wasn't one,' said Stripe firmly.

'You'd be surprised what a draught will do,' retorted his vast and feathery friend. 'I know them, because I live in a tall tree, and that's where you get all the best draughts. They creep about and wriggle in and nudge their way through the least-likely cracks and crannies. And if your candle-flame is just in the wrong position—near a tiny crack in the lantern door, for instance—out it'll go—pooff!'

Old Stripe regarded Woo deedily, the cup in his paw hovering uncertainly between his chest-level and his furry old face, waiting to be sipped at. At last, after having weighed the Owl's words very carefully and working out what he had just said about draughts and cracks and all that sort of such he said humbly:

'You really think so, Woo Owl?'

Woo Owl lifted his wings in an expressive gesture and said again—'Poooff!'

Skip Squirrel sat fascinated by Owl's chin-feathers as they fluttered up and down on the stalks, every time he said 'poooff!' in a loud and definite tone. But the small brown folk wasn't satisfied.

'What about my milk going sour?' he asked. *That* would make him think.

It did. And after he'd thought, Owl said simply:

'My dear Skip Squirrel. It's high Summer-time. Therefore it's exceeding hot. Therefore your milk will undoubtedly turn sour, seeing that your larder faces south. Have you ever thought of that?'

Skip Squirrel grew very small and brown and quiet while he thought of his larder facing south, and what it meant, and especially what it would mean to milk, in a sour-making manner.

'You think it's because of that?'

Woo waved an airy wing-tip and looked very superior.

'Has the milk turned sour since the three days you told me about?' he asked gently.

'No,' said Skip.

'There you are, then!'

'Because I've drunk it before it had time.'

Owl sat back, slightly nonplussed. He glanced at Stripe.

'What about your lantern, Stripey? Has that been going out since the time you mention?'

'No,' said Stripe, 'to be honest.'

Woo nodded largely. 'Exactly,' he said.

'But then I've never lit it, since then. It annoyed me too much.'

Woo Owl sought round for a defence against this argument; but long before he'd found one, Potter was talking about his water-wheel and the tricks it played on him; and Scruff Fox was waxing loud upon the misbehaviour of his bonfire.

Woo Owl managed, at last, to convince his friends, as they sat supping his coffee and munching his cakes. He summed up by saying:

'Old Stripe, you obviously had a stray draught lurking in your lantern. Skip Squirrel—any milk will go sour in the sun. Scruff Fox, you just don't know how to build a bonfire that burns, for all your experience. Potter, the sooner you clear those weeds away from your water-wheel, the sooner it's going to stop playing tricks on you.'

They looked at him in silence, wondering a little what they'd been making all the fuss about. Their friend the Owl was the wisest folk in all the Woodland, and what he didn't know about things wasn't worth looking up in his collection of Ancient and Learned Books.

'Well, we're sorry to have bothered you, I'm sure,' Old Stripe spoke for all of them. 'And we're very glad you've been able to set our minds at rest. We must tell all the other folk that there's a simple reason for their little troubles.'

'We certainly must,' nodded Potter, very relieved about his water-wheel.

'We'll go round first thing in the morning,' piped up Skip Squirrel, mightily glad that there hadn't really been any mysterious hobgoblins tunring his milk to cheese.

Woo Owl smiled on his good friends benignly in the bright candle-light, nodding his big feathery head and making small clucking-sounds of calm contentment with his beak. He loved his good neighbours well, and was more than fond of their cheerful company; but really they were just a little bit—well—simple . . .

'Then we can forget all about it,' he said, 'and talk of more sensible things. I've been thinking, lately, you know, of an idea that came to me—'

He didn't finish. Whatever his idea had been about, his friends certainly didn't manage to hear of it at the moment. Because without any warning at all, the door of the room came bursting open and the handle came flying off, to rattle and scamper along the floor until it landed against the leg of Owl's chair after catching his foot a nimble bump on his most tender corn.

Even as the folk around him got to their feet in alarm, every single candle went out, leaving them in pitchy darkness.

Yet there was no wind, no sound, no movement of anything but the door. In the silence and the darkness, Potter-the-Otter whispered nervously:

'I—I suppose that was one of your little draughts, Woo Owl . . . '

But Woo Owl said nothing. For one thing he was rubbing his foot where the door-knob had bumped it; and for another thing he was now quite convinced that his friends were *right*. There was magic in the Wood, and it had found his house at last.

Chapter 3

The Strange Blue Lights

MOLE-THE-MILLER walked alone along the woodland path from Badger's Beech, his large pink paws clasped behind his little round velvety back, and his small pink nose pointing towards the ground as he thought about deep and deedy problems. All the folk of the Wood had talked the day long of the curious things that had been going on among the trees; but still Skip Squirrel didn't know why his milk had turned sour; and still Potter didn't have the answer to his waterwheel and its little tricks.

Mole couldn't make head or tail of it, but he didn't give up trying to. At this moment, he knew vaguely that his feet were taking him in the direction of his home, the snug dwelling on Heather Hill that had the heather itself as a roof, and rooms far below the well-loved slopes. But if an idea came to his mind, more than likely he'd be off in a quite different direction.

And it was when he was thinking of Sweethallow Valley, and of the folk who dwelled there, that his feet *did* change their direction.

The Strange Blue Lights

'I wonder,' he wondered to himself, 'if those folk have had any trouble in the Valley?'

And he went on wondering, while his feet took him firmly along a path to the east, where the Wild River wound its twilight way between the sleeping willows.

'I wonder,' he mused with half his velvety mind, 'where I seem to be off to now, of such a sudden?' And he lifted his nose to see where he was a-going. 'Of course. I'm going to see the Valley dwellers. They might tell me something that will help.'

So he reached the river, and turned along the pathway and finally crossed the old rustic bridge, somewhere between Otter's Island and Marten's Elm. Not long after he left the East bank of the river, he found the pathway leading suddenly downwards, and the next moment he was lost to sight, from any who happened to be watching him from the Wood, as he descended the sharp slopes where the pine trees reared, their heads already crowned with mist as night came softly through the Valley.

Most of the folk lived right in the bottom, so that they had water nearby for their houses; but one or two of the Gray Squirrels dwelled higher on the hills, and the house nearest to Deep Wood belonged to a certain Squirrel by name Old Tufty (for he was old and his tail was probably the tuftiest in the land).

Miller Mole looked up as he walked, his small

black eyes searching the twilight for the tree-dwelling that was his destination. The Deep Woodlanders and the Sweethallow Folk usually kept themselves much to themselves; but relations between them were by no means unfriendly, and once or twice a folk of the trees would make a neighbourly call on a folk of the valley; and sometimes it would be the other way round.

Mole knew that Old Tufty would probably be in, so late at night, so now he peered into the half-light for the gleam of windows in the tree-trunk where he had his house.

Just as Mole rounded a bend in the pathway and saw the Valley spread before him as a deep blue chasm, something caught his eye, and he stopped dead.

It was a soft blue light. For a moment he had thought it was one of Old Tufty's windows, as the little house must be quite close by now. But there were two things about this soft blue light that made it appear not at all like one of Tufty's windows.

For one thing it was blue. As blue as a summer cornflower.

For another thing it moved. Gently, silently, soft as a thistledown along the breeze, it moved among the trees; and Mole the Miller watched it, holding his little black velvety breath.

Certainly he was near Tufty's house in the pine tree, for he could smell the smoke of apple-logs in the air, which meant that the Gray Squirrel was cooking himself a kettle of tea before bed-time. But this strange lantern that appeared to float in the air was certainly nothing to do with the Squirrel's house.

'Well bless my velvet . . . ' murmured Mole, and stroked his chest in wonderment. He stood watching the light until, with a mischievous wink, it went out; and there was nothing but the gathering gloom of nightfall. Mole felt suddenly lonely and very small indeed. Above him reared the gigantic timbers, their branches spread like slumbering clouds against the stars. Below him lay the great blue depths of the valley, parts of it shrouded in mist that was creeping from the stream and over the meadows. Here and there a pale light gleamed from a window or a porchway; but there was no sound, until—until suddenly Mole listened with all his attention.

Faintly, faintly he heard the distant whispering of strange voices; voices he had never known before in all his days. They carried to him across the sloping ground, as though a zephyr bore them to his tingling ears. Yet there was no zephyr, nor did any single leaf move upon its bough, however frail.

'They're the Valley dwellers,' he murmured, perhaps to hear the sound of his own voice for comfort. 'Talking on their way home from some feasting or other.'

The Strange Blue Lights

But Mole-the-Miller knew, deep inside him, that these were no ordinary voices of Squirrels or Chipmunks. They were too faint, too soft, too airy for ordinary tongues in furry cheeks.

Mole gave a sudden shiver, and his feet went put-put-put along the pathway as he hurried for the pine where lived his sometime friend Old Tufty. The trees were too tall for Mole; they towered above him, mighty and mysterious with their crowns of mist and their great black boughs held huge against the skies. The shadows were too dark for Mole; they crept, they waited for his coming, they hid the ground about him and sought to lead him off the path.

And there was that strange blue light, drifting through the air; and there were those mysterious voices, chanting their unearthly music among the shrouded trees.

The little black folk almost gasped with relief as he saw the first warm-lit window of the Gray Squirrel's house, seeming to beckon a welcome to him from the pine tree. In a moment he was climbing the short wooden ladder to the front door, and knocking impatiently. For a while there was no answer, no sound from within the house, until suddenly a window was thrown open just above Mole's head, and a voice said:

'You can just go away again!'

Mole lifted his head and peered into the shadows.

'I beg pardon?' he enquired mildly.

'And if ye don't go before I count three, then I'll be down there with me broom to sweep you off that porch of mine!'

Mole blinked. He recognised the Gray Squirrel's voice; but this wasn't quite the same sort of welcome he usually received from his neighbour of the valley. But then you never knew what folk would change into if their mood took them. One day they'd be all over you and the next day they'd pass you in the Wood without so much as a how-d'ye-do. Mole sighed. He used to like the old Gray Squirrel a lot. Most everyone liked Old Tufty, and Old Tufty liked most everyone. It was a very great pity.

He was just going to make his humble way off Old Tufty's porch when it occurred to him that it was possible there might be some little error. At least it was worth trying.

'This—this is me,' he remarked gently, looking up at the dim shape of Old Tufty's head.

'I know it's you!' retorted the Gray Squirrel, 'and I've seen a deal too much of ye already. Be off!'

Mole-the-Miller gave a deep sigh inside of his small black velvet chest, and turned sadly away from the front door. He was feeling most and unconscionably lonely, was Mole-the-Miller. All around him stood the great pines; and below him was spread the mysterious Valley, wreathed in mist and shadowed in the shrouds of night. It was a long way home to Heather Hill, and the way was dark, for the stars gave little light.

And there were those strange unearthly voices in the trees; and that queer blue light that drifted through the air . . .

Desperately Mole-the-Miller turned again and looked up at the window where Tufty's head still showed.

'Are—are you sure you know what sort of Me this is?' he asked timidly, hoping the Gray Squirrel did, and hoping he still liked small Moles who lived in Mills.

'What's your name?' snapped the voice above him.

Mole trembled unhappily.

'M-m-mole,' he said simply.

'*Who?*'

'I —I'm the M-m-miller,' said Mole hopefully, hoping Old Tufty still liked flour.

Whether Old Tufty still liked flour, and whether he still liked Moles who lived in Mills, he didn't say at the moment.

Mole heard the window slam; then there were faint but loudening footsteps, as though Tufty was coming down his stairs with as little delay as possible; then—so abruptly that Mole drew back in mild alarm—the front door was opened with a jerk, and the Gray Squirrel stood there, silhouetted against the cosy light of the hall and holding a large broom in his paw.

For a moment he peered at his visitor, holding the broom as though he were more than ready to begin his threat of sweeping him off the porch; then his voice squeaked excitedly:

'Well, well, well! If it isn't Mole-the-Miller, bless me whiskers!'

'Well it *is* Mole-the-Miller,' said Mole nervously, 'but bless your whiskers, just the same.'

'Come in, come in, do!' piped Old Tufty, dropping his broom against the wall and holding out his paws. 'This *is* a surprise!'

Mole followed him inside, shaking his paw warmly.

'It was a surprise for me, too,' he murmured; but his little warm heart beat faster, and there was a pleasant glow in his chest. It had all been a dreadful mistake . . .

'You must have thought me out of me wits,' went on Old Tufty, leading the way to his cosy sitting-room. 'I hadn't any idea it was a friend of mine on the front porch.'

He settled Mole in his best chair, which was specially comfortable for visitors, and was soon working his kettle up into a proper state for making tea with.

'Have a pipe of baccy, my dear Miller,' he offered cheerfully. 'Help yourself, do—plenty in the tobacco-jar on the mantelpiece there. Got your tinder-box? How d'ye like your tea, strong, weak, not too much milk, how much sugar?'

Mole-the-Miller basked in this friendly company as Old Tuft pottered confortably about, getting the tea ready and asking his guest for news of the Wood on the western side of the Wild River.

'And how's Old Stripe a-getting along? And Potter, and Woo Owl?'

He sat down at last, drawing his chair nearer Mole's, so they could both gaze from the quaint little window to where the lights of the Valley dwellers winked fitfully below them.

When Mole judged his friend had exhausted his conversation for a while, he said:

'Old Stripe is pothered.'

'Pothered?'

Mole nodded, and told the old Gray Squirrel about the Badger and his bother. After which he told him about Potter and his water-wheel. And when he'd told the story of all the queer and curious happenings of the Wood, he said:

'So on my way home, I thought I'd call and see you. It's one of the pleasant-most things I know, calling on you is, and I wondered if you'd had any similar occurrences a-going on down here in the Valley.'

Gray Squirrel looked at Mole, and said 'Tch!' Then he rolled his wide brown eyes at the ceiling, looked at Mole again and said 'Tch!' Then he pursed his whiskers and said: 'My, my—I should think we *have* had some bother!'

'Ah,' said Mole, in his most interested tone.

'Not the same sort of thing,' went on Old Tufty, 'but every bit as bothersome. They began about three nights ago.'

Mole glanced at him.

'They?' he murmured.

Tuft nodded vigorously.

'The Hobgoblins,' he said.

'Who?' asked Mole. He was sitting very still, and not a single whisker moved as he gazed at his host.

'The Hobgoblins,' repeated Old Tufty, 'or whatever you like to call them. They might be Sprites or Elves or Imps or Leprechauns, I'm sure I don't know. But they're certainly about the place.'

'What—exactly are they?' enquired Mole, who didn't know.

Tufty shrugged. 'No one really can tell. All we can see is a lot of queer blue lights, floating about in—'

'Aaahhh!' cried Mole.

Old Tufty blinked nervously.

'I've seen one,' nodded the Miller. 'Just as I was coming down to call on you tonight. A little blue light that was like a thistledown drifting along.'

'That's the sort of thing!' agreed the Squirrel.

'That was one of 'em! And that's how they came to the Valley. All we saw of them was—' he broke off.

'Yes?' said Mole.

Tufty was gazing from the window, watching something far below in the depths of the Valley. After a moment he got up, opened the window wide, and beckoned to the Miller.

'There you are—you can see them for yourself!'

Mole leaned on the window-seat and stared into the distance, where mists rolled silently in the pale starlight. Then he saw them. A string of those soft blue lights, moving across the Valley as though a score of thistledowns, each lit with a blue candle, were drifting in the air, following one another between the trees, in and out of the little houses and chalets, diving sometimes to skim above the pale flowing ripples of the stream, rising sometimes to ring the highest pine-trees with their mazy circling.

'They—they look like Will-o'-the-Wisps!' breathed Mole softly.

'They may be,' shrugged the Squirrel. 'Call 'em what you will, but they're a nuisance.'

'Do they speak?' asked Mole, remembering those strange and elfin voices in the trees.

'Do they *speak!*' echoed Old Tufty. 'My—you should just hear them when they sit on your chimneys!'

'S-sit on the ch-chimneys?'

'Of course! That's how we first knew about them.'

The Strange Blue Lights

Old Tufty gazed at the wreathing blue lights a moment more, then he said 'let's make ourselves comfy again and have a pipe, while I tell you of them.'

So Mole-the-Miller settled down again into the arm-chair, and filled the little black bowl of his briar pipe with some of the Gray Squirrel's tobacco. And when they'd got their pipes burning well, Tufty leaned back in his chair, blew out a plume of blue clover-smoke, and said:

'The first one to know about the Goblins was young Joe Chipmunk, who lives near the stream. He was sitting to sup one night when he heard such a shindy going on, somewhere above his chimneys. At first he thought some Birds had perched there, and were having an argument; but when he went out to look up at his roof, there they were—a score of Hobgobblies, dancing and jigging round and round the chimneys, chattering and chanting until he thought he was in Monkeyland!'

Mole listened, and was quiet with amaze.

'Then,' nodded Old Tufty, 'when young Joe Chipmunk made to chase them off, what did they do but swoop down and chase him back into his own house! Had to slam the door on 'em or they'd have been inside after him!'

Mole-the-Miller boggled, and his pipe went out in alarm.

'Then it all began,' went on the old Gray Squirrel,

scratching his tinder and relighting his tobacco. 'The Goblins went about the Valley, up and down, round all the houses, chattering and singing until none of us could get any sleep the night long. We held a meeting and decided to give as good as they gave. Wherever they went, we chased 'em with sticks and stones! Whenever we thought we could catch 'em, we tried—but you think they'd let us? It was like trying to catch a candle-beam!'

Little black Mole sat unmoving, listening to the amazing tale Old Tufty was telling him.

'Now it's a little better,' the Squirrel finished. 'They still fly over the houses and they still sing sometimes at night. But they never come near any of us, because they know we're ready. Maybe they'll tire of their tricks before long. I've noticed, sometimes, how they go off over the top o' the hills, to pester other folks' lands. Often we don't see them for a long while, and then they're back, haunting our trees again.'

He looked very apologetically at Mole-the-Miller, and added: 'That's why I told you I'd sweep you off me doorstep when you called tonight. Not many folk knock at this time o' night, you see, an' it's one of the Hobgoblin's tricks. They'll knock on your door, and when it's opened ye'll see nothing but their impish blue lamps, mocking at ye from the darkness!'

Mole-the-Miller sat nodding, and lit his pipe

again, and thought a very great deal about all he had heard from his host. Then he said:

'Now we *know* . . . '

'What do we know, Miller-Mole?'

'Where they go off to, when they leave the Valley sometimes.'

Old Tufty bobbed his head in agreement. 'They've been at your milk and your water-wheels and such.' He wagged his head seriously, 'You folk in the Wood will just have to do the same as we did—chase 'em!'

'But we never see them!' complained Mole. 'Even in the darkness we've never seen their blue lamps.'

'Then they're trying different tricks in different ways. They're putting something sour in the milk before you can so much as turn round; they're swimming under the ripples of the river and pulling at Potter's wheel—and when he dives in, they're away like a flash!'

Mole-the-Miller rose to his feet, and drew himself up to his full height until he stood as tall as a primrose-clump. If the Valley dwellers could subdue the Hobgoblins, then surely the Wood-landers could . . .

'I'm going straight back to tell the others,' he declared boldly, 'before there's more mischief done.'

So Old Tufty went with him as far as the Wild River (for Mole, brave as he was, seemed chary of going alone, even though he was too proud to say so). They parted on the bridge, and Mole went onwards over the winding pathway, remembering that Old Stripe and Skip and Scruff and Potter had said they would be going over to Owl's Beech, to see why Woo hadn't been at the meeting at the Badger's house. So Mole turned off the path close by Otter's Island, and made for Woo's Glade. There was little radiance from the skies to guide him; but he knew almost every tree in the woodland. Before he was prepared for it, he found himself in the shadowed glade, looking up at the great beech that towered above him.

In ordinary times it was a friendly tree, with more than one of its latticed windows winking a warm welcome below the crook of a branch or high among the leaves. There were so many rooms and circular stairways in the beech that a caller would nearly always see a window lit, or some smoke curling from one of the many chimneys.

But tonight the beech was silent, and no light gleamed from any room. No thread of smoke was woven against the stars. It was getting to be midnight, Mole knew well, so perhaps Owl had gone to bed. That couldn't be helped. He had news of the greatest importance for his friends. The word would have to be spread; and Woo, on his wide, swift wings, was the folk for spreading it.

Mole-the-Miller climbed the long rope-ladder

from the moss to the high front porch. The lantern was out; but that might mean that Woo had forgotten to light it. Usually it could be seen shining among the trees, to guide any traveller to a place where there was always a cup of something hot for him, and a fill of tobacco for his pipe, whatever the time of night.

'Well well,' murmured the Miller, as he reached the front door. He didn't quite know why he'd said 'well well,' but possibly it was to hear the sound of his own familiar and friendly voice. He lifted the knocker, and let it fall.

'Hum-hum-hum . . . ' he muttered, moving his feet up and down on the polished floor of the porch. 'I wonder if he is, or if he's not. Meaning in, of course, yes.'

But nobody came. The great house, high above the mossy floor of the glade, might well have been deserted, for there came no sight nor sound of any folk.

'Obviously fast asleep,' said Mole. But he was determined to rouse Woo Owl and all the Wood if necessary. The Hobgoblins had invaded their trees, and the alarm must be raised at once.

Mole raised the knocker and banged it down in the most alarming manner he knew. The sound of it echoed through the rambling house, as though a thunderclap had beat from the very heavens.

The Strange Blue Lights

Mole-the-Miller took his paws away from his ears, and listened. There was no sound of Woo Owl.

'Drat!' he declared. Obviously the absurd folk must be staying with Old Stripe for the night—as many of them did, for his hospitality was unequalled in the woodland. Now Mole didn't mind this at all, except for the dismal fact that he must now go all the way to Badger's Beech. Alone. In the dark. With no folk with him. All by his velvety self.

And Hobgoblins about in the trees.

'Tut-tut-tut,' said Mole, to keep his spirits up. He peered down into the gloom of Woo's Glade. It would be better to go down the ladder and just pop across to see the Badger, because Stripe was cheerful company, and would soon help him with his important news-spreading. On the other hand, the glade below looked rather dark and shadowy and murky and lurky; whereas this was a familiar and well-known tree. Here was Woo Owl's very own front porch, right beneath his feet. And this was Woo's lantern (out, it was true). And this was Woo's front door (shut, it was true).

'Oh dear . . . ' sighed Mole-the-Miller. He was really rather tired of being lonely and of wandering about by himself all night with a lot of mischievous Hobgobblies waiting to pounce on small and unwary Moles who chose to stray from home.

He was just making up his mind to brave the terrors of the trees and knock upon Old Stripe's door instead of Woo Owl's, in case it sounded to be a better noise, when a new idea occurred to him.

Something might have happened to Woo Owl.

He might be in the throes of an attack by the Goblins.

He might even—

But Mole-the-Miller stopped himself thinking too deeply about all the dreadful things that *might* be happening to his old feathered friend. Action was what he wanted.

The door-handle turned to his paw; and the door opened, its hinges shrieking eerily. (Folk had been telling Woo about his door-hinges ever since the house had been built in the tree.)

In the hall was a candle, leaning wearily from its holder on the wall. Mole looked at it in the light of his tinder, and then touched the wick. When the flame leapt brightly, he closed the front door behind him.

He'd take a quick peep into every room, to see if Owl were at home (and, if he were, if he were safe and sound), then he'd pop across to Badger's Beech to find Old Stripe.

His feet went pit-pit-pit over the polished parquet floor of the hall as he made his way to the sitting-room, the candle burning cheerfully in his paw. He was just going to open the door when—he didn't, instead.

For in his ears, quite plainly, he heard a strange

elfin chuckle of laughter. And in the same second, the candle-flame went out with a tiny hiss, leaving him in the pitchy darkness.

Something like an icicle crept down the back of Mole-the-Miller; and some very hot candle-wax splashed onto his paw. But the strangest thing was that when he dropped the candle in his alarm, it made no sound.

It was almost as though someone had caught it.

Mole-the-Miller was at the end of his wits.

In the great silence of the house, his small velvety voice was raised on high, reaching to the topmost rooms of all—

'Woo! Woo Owl! Where are you, Woo Owl?'

Eerily the echoes called back—

Woo Owl . . . Where are you, Woo Owl . . .?

Chapter 4

The Coming of the Great Wind

'I—I THINK I'd like to go home,' said Skip Squirrel, peering into the gloom of the room as he nudged himself a little nearer Old Stripe for comfort and moral support.

'I th-think I'll go with you,' murmured Potter, his eyes boggling round him in the murk.

Old Stripe didn't say nuffin. He didn't approve of all this queer sort of come-and-go; not in the least. Sitting comfortably in Woo's sun-parlour with his friends, talking to them in the bright candle-light, was a very very different thing from *this*. There was the horrid question, asking itself in their minds: *who opened the door just now?*

And there was another question, every bit as horrid: *who snuffed the candles?*

In the deep and serious silence, the voice of Woo Owl came to the ears of his guests:

'I must apologize,' he boomed formally. 'I assure you this is not my usual way of entertaining my friends.'

'I wouldn't be here,' said Skip unthinkingly, 'if it was.'

The Coming of the Great Wind

Woo Owl blinked in the gloom; but no-folk could see him.

'Something will have to be done,' said Old Stripe.

'Immediately,' said Potter, and sat rooted to his chair.

'Well, there you are, then,' said Scruff Fox, and wished he were nice and snug in his bed at Fox End.

'Hhrrccmmm . . . ' they heard Woo Owl, as he cleared his feathery throat. 'Don't be alarmed,' he warned them, 'I am about to rise.'

There was a gentle draught as he stood up and opened his wings to touch something familiar. On his left was a kind of warm lump, covered in fur. For a moment he stroked it in puzzlement.

'That,' suggested Old Stripe mildly, 'is my head.'

Woo blinked.

'Ah,' he said carefully. 'Then I must be facing the door.' He essayed a few short paces and fetched up smartly against a chair.

'Have a care,' murmured Potter.

'This is no time for having a chair, thank you Potter,' Owl rebuked him gently. 'I am about to get to the bottom of this curious affair. It would appear I made too light of your anxiety. Owl's Beech would seem to be as haunted as your own houses. I disapprove of that, most strongly.'

He found his way to the door, after draping a generous and exploring wing all over a very small

The Coming of the Great Wind

Skip Squirrel, who emerged in due course for breath.

'Ah,' remarked Owl, fumbling about.

'Ah what?' enquired Scruff Fox.

'I have discovered the tinder-box. I usually keep one handy, near the door.' There followed patient sounds of flint being struck, accompanied by sparks. When the tinder took flame, Woo Owl lit a candle, and blinked solemnly at his friends. They regarded him uneasily.

'What happens now?' enquired Scruff, thinking that almost anything might.

'I don't know,' said Old Stripe. 'But I shouldn't wonder if that candle goes out before we're very much older. They don't seem to last long, these nights.'

Woo observed his candle and noted with satisfaction its steady flame. With deliberate care, he loomed slowly round the room, lighting all the other candles in turn.

His friends looked more cheerful. Scruff Fox even went as far as to light his pipe up.

'Oh well,' he said, 'thank you for having me, Woo Owl. I think I'll be getting along.'

'Scruff Fox,' said Old Stripe, 'I'm surprised at you.'

'So am I,' nodded little Skip Squirrel, and looked at Old Stripe. 'Why?' he added.

'Here's our dear friend Woo,' frowned the

Badger, 'all alone in his house, with some sort of Mystery making itself and bursting doors open and blowing candles out—and all Scruff wants to do is to go home. It's shameful!'

Scruff Fox hung his head and let his pipe go out again in sheer shame. But, as he rightly said: 'I don't see what help I can be, Stripey. All one can do about a door is to shut it, after all, if it happens to be open. I'll do *that* with pleasure.'

Old Stripe was just trying to think out a suitable answer, as to other things that might be done about open doors, apart from closing them, when Woo Owl, who had been wandering about on the staircase, said:

'Phssstt!'

Skip Squirrel leaped into the air and came down quivering.

'Wh-what was th-th-that?' he asked Old Stripe, clutching his friendly brown paw.

'Hark!' persisted Woo from half-way down the stairs, 'I can hear something!'

'I know,' retorted Skip. 'I was asking Stripe what it—'

'Oh *do* be quiet a moment!' Woo interrupted him.

They were quiet. Old Stripe thought he heard a noise, but when he turned to see where it was coming from, he found it was old Potter, panting nervously through his whiskers. Scruff Fox was sure he heard a noise, too, but it was only Skip

Squirrel quivering from the tips of his tufty brown ears to the end of his bushy brown tail.

'There it goes again,' said Woo softly from the stairs.

Potter panted more vigorously, and Skip trembled like a junket in a draught.

'What sort of noise is it?' asked Stripe, creeping as quietly as he could towards the stairs.

'Very faint,' Woo told him. 'I think someone's climbing up the visiting-ladder to my front door.'

In the great silence of the house they strained their ears. Even had the slightest sound floated up to them, they would have heard it. As it was, there came a knock so sudden and so loud that Skip jumped clear of the floor and Potter made a noise like a violin on his whiskers and Old Stripe said:

'Bless my stripes!'

'There you are,' nodded Woo, his wing-tip shaking a little as he held the candle above him. 'A caller!'

'Tell him to go away, then,' said Skip.

'It might be a friend of ours.' Woo began descending the stairs slowly.

'Don't risk it,' said Potter simply.

Woo gave himself a moment to ponder. Great though his determination was, he cared little for the idea of going down to open his front door, without first discovering the identity of his caller.

He was about to make up his feathery old mind

when a noise so shattering rose from his front-door-knocker that he gave an involuntary hoot of alarm.

When the power of speech returned to Scruff Fox, he said:

'No folk of the kind *we* know ever knock on a folk's door like *that*.'

'Was it a knock?' asked Woo unhappily, 'or were they breaking it down?'

'They didn't have much trouble with this one,' Skip reminded him. He gripped Old Stripe's comforting paw even harder. He didn't care for this sort of skulduggery at all. Deep Wood had been a friendly, peaceful place before Black Magic had come to visit the trees by night.

'I am about to enquire into these Noises,' announced Woo Owl at last. 'Will anyone come with me?'

Skip Squirrel was as quiet as ever he'd been in all his furry young life.

Potter-the-Otter gave a careful cough, which excused him from answering.

Scruff Fox looked into the bowl of his pipe, frowning over the sudden and unexpected problem of its having gone out.

'I will,' said Old Stripe.

'Then I will, too,' declared Potter, rallying to the call.

'I don't see why all of us shouldn't go,' remarked Scruff, still slightly ashamed of his previous lack of response. 'Do you, Skip Squirrel?'

The Coming of the Great Wind

Skip Squirrel said he certainly didn't see why they all shouldn't; so Woo Owl nodded importantly and took a cautious step farther down the stairs.

'I,' he announced largely, 'shall lead.'

They searched the landing below the sun-parlour, and Woo lit more candles as they went. But there was nothing to be seen, or heard, or felt, or even guessed at.

'I suppose,' murmured Old Stripe, as they reached the kitchen, 'no one knows what we're looking for?'

'I daren't imagine,' said Skip.

'We are looking—' began Woo Owl, speaking slowly to give himself time to think what they *were* looking for—'we are looking, my friends—' and again he broke off.

'We know we're *looking*,' nodded Stripe simply. 'But what we want to know is what *for*?'

Owl said nothing. Except: 'pssstt!'

They did.

And then they heard what Owl had heard. A soft pit-pit-pit of small footsteps, on the other side of the sitting-room door.

Skip Squirrel ducked nimbly under one of Woo's large and sheltering wings. Potter-the-Otter boggled at the sitting-room door. Scruff Fox said 'tch-tch-tch!' under his breath by way of keeping the conversation going. Old Stripe was just going to say something comforting, when he was interrupted long before he could get it out.

The Coming of the Great Wind

In the deep silence of the house there came suddenly a voice that was raised to its highest pitch—

'*Woo! Woo Owl! Where are you, Woo Owl?*'

They were petrified.

'Who's that?' gasped Owl, waving his shaking candle in the direction of the sitting-room.

'I think he's asking for you,' suggested Stripe blandly, trying to steady his paws.

'Has anything happened yet?' came the muffled tones of little Skip Squirrel, who was still deep in the shelter of a large and friendly wing.

He was jerked off his feet as Woo took a determined stride into the sitting-room, crossed it, and opened the door.

64

The Coming of the Great Wind

Whatever Woo had been expecting, it was not the small black, velvety, barrel-shaped form who hurled himself into the first pair of vast and protective wings he came to. And they happened to belong to Woo.

'It—it *can't* be!' stuttered Potter.

'Oh *good!*' said Skip Squirrel, from the muffling confines of the long curtains. He didn't know who 'it' was; but Potter sounded glad about something.

'It's—Mole-the-Miller!' gasped Scruff Fox, his pipe dropping from his chin.

'Is it?' said a small velvet voice as Mole emerged from his protective pair of wings. He blinked in the candle-light, and stroked himself smooth again. 'I—I mean of course it is, yes. Me—Mole, that's who he is. I mean that's who—'

'We're glad to see you,' announced Owl, the perfect host.

'That certainly goes for me,' Mole assured him.

'My dear Mole—come along into the kitchen and we'll make some coffee. What were you shouting for?'

'You,' said Mole, as they followed their large host into his cosy round kitchen. 'I was wanting to know if you were in.' He looked round at all his friends while his little heart stopped racing and his eyes blinked more and more happily with every blink as he gazed at familiar and well-loved things. Here was Woo Owl's great gleaming dresser, stacked with blue china and tobacco-jars and soup-plates and all manner of crockery, just as it had always been. And here were his own good friends, all of them wanting to make him some coffee. Mole felt most and exceeding happy of a sudden, and a small bright tear of relief trickled from his eye and all the way down his long pink nose, where it glistened at the very tip until it fell and was gone forever.

He sniffed politely, and added: 'beg pardon, I'm sure.' Already he was feeling rather ashamed of his outburst in the hall. But he could still remember that elfin chuckle of laughter, and the tiny hiss of the candle as the flame had been snuffed by Someone.

'Yes,' he said, watching Woo put the kettle on the hob. 'I wondered if you were in, that's all.'

Woo glanced at his small velvet friend.

'You certainly seemed to be determined to find out,' he nodded slowly. 'We heard the front door collapsing, and—'

'Oh,' said Mole, watching the coffee being stirred into the milk, 'that was just knocking. I'll tell you all about it.'

'We heard,' remarked Stripe, whose ears were still singing.

'All about *everything*!' said Mole, now trembling more with the excitement of his story than with the fright he had had in the hall.

'Then let us be seated,' suggested Owl largely. 'Old Stripe, would you have the kindness to get some cups? Potter, old chap, where's the sugar?'

The Coming of the Great Wind

They got the cups and the sugar and put the tray on the table and Owl poured the rich golden coffee while Mole-the-Miller made a series of small polite coughing-tones to prepare himself for his speech. And when everyone was drinking from his steaming cup, Mole told his tale.

'So *that's* what it's all about!' said Stripe, when the story was done.

'Hobgoblins!' said Potter, his whiskers trembling at the thought. 'Playing about with my water-wheel!'

'Leprechauns in my milk!' said Skip indignantly.

'Will-o'-the-Wisps in my lantern!' growled the Badger, and drew grimly on his pipe.

'Wait till I get my garden-broom on their rascally young backs!' cried Scruff Fox. 'I'll give 'em bonfire!'

The Deep Woodlanders were roused. There was magic in the trees, but nothing that they couldn't deal with. If the folk of Sweethallow had got the best of them, then the Woodlanders were more than their match!

'How do we tackle them?' asked Scruff, looking to Woo for guidance. Woo would know. He had Ancient and Learned Books in his smoking-room below the stairs. There was bound to be something about Sprites in one of them.

'Just as the Valley folk did!'

'No!' said Mole, and shook his head. 'The Valley

folk could see them, because of their blue lamps. *We* can't. I never caught a glimpse of the one in the hall just now, but he was certainly there.'

'That's right,' nodded Stripe slowly. 'When there's been mischief, we've never seen anything, true.'

'Then I shall consult my Tomes,' declared Woo Owl largely.

'I beg pardon?' suggested Mole.

'My Tomes,' said Woo, 'by which I mean my Learned Books.'

'Oh,' said Mole; and they waited for Owl to go and fetch them. He rose from the company, steered himself importantly in the direction of his study under the stairs, and was about to launch his portly and feathered person across the kitchen, when a window flew open, with startling suddenness.

'It's the wind, this time,' called Potter, as he got up and closed it. 'I told you there was one rising.'

Woo Owl gazed at the window suspiciously, remembering how the door of the sun-parlour had burst open not long ago. But he could glimpse the stars, glinting fitfully through the leaves, as the branches moved to the wind's first gusts.

He was coming back to the kitchen with three enormous volumes under his left wing, when another window flew open to a mighty gust of wind that hissed through the boughs outside.

68

The Coming of the Great Wind

'Going to be a squall!' cried Scruff Fox, and forced the casement closed.

Other folk may have said other things, but their voices were lost in the sudden welter of sound as the wind came with a new fury, dragging with great wings at the branches and echoing through the lofty timbers of the beech. Woo Owl and his friends were aghast at the temper of it as another window came flying open and banged against the wall even as a plate toppled from the dresser and crashed into pieces on the floor, while the whole tree trembled to the onslaught of the raging gale that now stormed through the Wood, bellowing among the glades and driving the leaves still green from the boughs before its furied strength.

As the folk in Woo's Beech stared from the windows into the glade below, there came stars, suddenly, scattering and shining through the trees— blue stars, that glittered in the night as though the wind had torn them from the skies and was spilling them among the shadows of the earth.

'The Hobgoblins!' cried Mole, above the sound of the gale—'look—the Goblins are coming!'

His friends were silent, their tongues stilled by the sight of the mazing lights as they were whisked and tossed on the wings of the wind, wreathing and threading between the trees—and high, high above the voice of it there now sounded the Goblin choir, singing and chanting and mocking every ear that heard them as they drove through the witching wood.

The Sprites had left Sweethallow, and were come to the Wood with the wind.

Chapter 5

Hedgehog the Traveller

THAT night, when the Great Wind came to the Wood, Old Stripe and his friends the Fox, the Squirrel, the Otter and the Mole, stayed with their host, at Owl's Beech.

Clearly something must be done immediately, now that the Sprites had shown themselves in their true colours. The gale that brought them to the darkling trees was hushed to a wind and then to a breeze, before ten minutes had gone by. But the Imps remained, circling among the glades and spinneys, sending their elfin laughter echoing in quiet places—and sending many a woodland folk to listen at his chimney, where the voices floated down.

Woo Owl, slow and deedy that he was in ordinary times, rose magnificently to this critical occasion.

As soon as the wind had died, and the leaves were still again on every starlit bough, his voice boomed softly in the kitchen; and such was the attention he received, that even the cups and saucers on the dresser seemed to listen; and certainly the kettle stopped singing on the hearth.

'I think we might all adjourn to my study,' he

announced solemnly. 'If you folk would do me the honour, I suggest we all stay the night here, to work upon our plans. I shall see that an appropriate feast shall be provided, so that we may deliberate carefully over a tankard of ale, and later seek our pipes for wisdom and enlightenment.'

Skip Squirrel blinked nervously. Old Woo was using one or two words he didn't quite understand; and a few more he had never even heard of. So he hoped he wasn't going to be left out of anything through his ignorance.

Woo nodded slowly, satisfied with the impression he had made so far. Even Scruff Fox appeared to be paying attention, although his pipe had gone out and needed fiddling with.

'Old Stripe,' went on their large and portly host, 'would you consider making the front door your own especial responsibility?'

Old Stripe furrowed his brow.

'I mean,' explained Woo, 'if our Beech comes under any kind of attack by the Goblins, would you take care of the front door?'

'By all means,' nodded the Badger, though by what means he didn't quite know. What did one do to repel an Imp?

'I shall pass round some stout staves in a moment,' said Woo, understanding the Badger's problem.

'I wish I'd brought my garden-broom with me,' muttered Scruff Fox grimly. '*I'd* sweep 'em!'

Hedgehog the Traveller

'Then would you man the back door, Scruff Fox?'

Scruff Fox said he'd most certainly man the back door. Skip volunteered for the kitchen windows; Potter for the sitting-room windows; and Mole-the-Miller said he'd stand by to help which ever folk came in need of some.

Woo Owl nodded his satisfaction.

'If we hear anything of the rascals, then, we'll be ready for them! Now let us adjourn to my study.'

They all moved, except Skip, who didn't know what 'adjourn' really meant. When he saw what folk were a-doing, he wondered why Woo couldn't have used the simpler word 'go'; but then Woo was a wise old folk, and maybe the longer word meant 'go before it's too late,' or 'one by one' or 'mind you don't tread on my tail.'

When the door of the cosy room was closed, Woo Owl sat down importantly at the little round table, in the centre of whose rich and polished surface there stood a large candle in its holder. A few small logs were thrown into the hearth, as the night air was inclined to be chilly with the slow mist that was rising; and candles were lit all round the oak-panelled walls.

Every folk took his pipe and filled it from the large tobacco-bowl on the table; and before long there drifted upwards in the firelight the sweet blue smoke of clover and of thyme, to wreathe fragrantly among the ancient beams.

'First of all,' began Woo, blinking seriously before him, 'we must warn every Woodlander in the land. Now how shall we do that?'

'Ah,' said Old Stripe, to give himself time to think.

'Erm . . . ' murmured Potter, for the same reason.

'Ring a bell,' suggested Skip brightly.

'We have no bell,' remarked Owl.

'Shout "Fire"!' said Scruff Fox.

'Our voices would not carry,' Owl told him. 'Besides, we want to spread the news without the Sprites knowing. By stealth.'

'Stealth,' nodded Skip, liking the worldly sound of the word.

They pondered for a long time about how to spread things in a stealthy manner, and by the time no one had thought of anything, Owl said suddenly:

'Ah.'

Their heads turned to look at him.

'I shall fly,' he declared.

'Where?' asked Potter, who was not very quick.

'We shall write small messages,' intoned Woo deedily, working out his plan as he went along. 'On parchment.'

'And drop them down folks' chimneys!' said Stripe, who had just thought of it. Woo stared at him.

'Brilliant!' he boomed.

Hedgehog the Traveller

Old Stripe looked modestly at the table. But Scruff Fox had a frown.

'That's going to take you till dawn,' he said to Woo. For there were many folk in the Wood, when all were counted.

Woo blinked largely, and scratched the top of one of his feathery ears to help him over this little snag. His expression brightened suddenly.

'Then I shall ask the help of the Jackdaws!' he said. 'They live only a few trees away from here.'

'And the Woodpeckers!' said Skip Squirrel.

'And the Magpies!' nodded Potter, not to be left out.

So the task was begun, at once. Within an hour, Woo Owl took off from his doorstep, to glide on silent wings across the starlit glade, making for the elms where lived the Jackdaws. In Owl's Beech, his friends waited for him to return with his team of messengers. On the table in the study lay the pile of small parchment notices, reading simply:

> *Deep Woodlanders Biware! The Hobglobins are hear! Bolt your dores— Bare your windos—be reddy to risist attack! If overwelmed, get a messege to Owl's Beech, and help will be sent at onse!*

Woo had become entangled occasionally in the blackberry ink; and once or twice his spelling had displayed signs of confusion—but then he was in an urgent hurry, and there was no time to be lost in attention to such trivial details.

No one in the room was admiring these notices, for there were no candles burning. The house was in darkness, according to plan. The big study-window was wide open, to allow Woo and the other Birds to enter; and if candles were burning, the sprites might see, and make an attack before the messengers could begin their various journeys through the trees.

Old Stripe jumped nervously, prepared though he was, as Woo Owl landed with scarcely a sound of his soft-beating wings, his feet planted firmly on the window-sill.

'All ready, Stripe!' he called in a boomy whisper.

Potter-the-Otter passed the notices to the Badger, who gave them quickly to Owl, who handed them to the Jackdaws and Woodpeckers and Magpies waiting outside among the boughs.

In less than a minute, the folk in the room were hearing the soft movement of wings as the messengers took off, one by one, to vanish among the shadows of the leaves. Woo, the last to go, called over his shoulder—'Close the window!'— and he was away, diving silently to the airy spaces of the starlit glade, already making for the nearest neighbour, the old Hare who dwelled deep in Hare Burrow.

The Badger shut the window fast, and two

candles were lit, so that the Birds could see their gleam as they made back for home after their desperate errand in the Wood.

The folk who could not fly settled down to wait and to wonder, their thoughts following Owl and

his convoy of friends as they winged their silent way among the glades and spinneys, flitting in the shadows of giant beeches, diving to the tangled undergrowth to seek the home of a Rabbit or a Mole.

'Oh well,' Old Stripe murmured as he stuffed his pipe with new tobacco, 'there's nothing more to be done, until they come back.'

'Then we'll get them a meal ready,' suggested Potter-the-Otter. He attempted to sound very generous and unselfish about this; but his friends knew him too well.

'Potter-the-Otter,' remarked Scruff Fox mildly, 'I sometimes wonder how you manage to stand upright, after all the food you tuck away.'

Potter-the-Otter regarded him indignantly from the chair in which he sat.

'I was just thinking they'll be hungersome when they get back, *that's* all I was thinking.'

'Then I'll go and have a look round Woo's kitchen,' nodded Scruff simply, 'and fix a little feast for them, while you stay here and think of some more kind thoughts.' And off he went, taking Skip Squirrel with him to help work out some recipes and such.

'You know, Potter,' said Old Stripe, when they were left by themselves with Mole-the-Miller, 'I've been thinking.'

'Ah,' said Potter, wishing he were in the kitchen instead of in here listening to Badger's thinking.

'What sort?' enquired Mole, dangling his short plump legs from the settle-seat round the hearth, where a low fire of cherry-logs was glowing.

'About Hedgehog,' explained the Badger, still

peering deedily at the smoke that rose tranquilly from his pipe.

'Which one?' asked Potter—for there were a few in the Wood.

'Old Candles,' said Stripe. His two friends glanced at him. 'Old Candles' was their name for the little traveller who visited the wood with every season,

bringing them candles for their homes. No one in the land knew the secret of making them; but the old Hedgehog did. In Spring and Summer and Autumn he would come with his barrow, trundling it through the trees, loaded with pure-white glistening candles; and in Winter, when the first snows came whirling from the north, his barrow would be piled with coloured ones—amber and blue, green and shining crimson—so that the festive-boards would be decked with their gay bright hues beneath their crocus-flames.

No one knew where the Hedgehog lived; no one knew where he went; they knew only that he loved the Wood, and was loved himself by the dwellers in the trees. His every visit was a day for high occasion, and every door in the land was open to him.

'Old Candles . . .' nodded Potter-the-Otter, and he looked at Stripe with a frown. 'He'll be here, any day now!'

'Or any night,' said the Mole, his velvet face puckered by a frown of worry similar to the Otter's. No-folk knew when the traveller would arrive—for he seldom knew himself. His road was long and winding, and he bothered with Time not at all. If he came to the borders of the Wood by night, then he'd more than likely curl up and sleep beneath a hedge, rather than disturb his friends until morning.

'What about the Hobgoblins?' said Stripe; and these words expressed their thoughts aloud.

Potter blew angrily through his whiskers.

'They'll attack him, if they're in the Wood!'

'They'll see him coming,' nodded Mole vigorously, 'alone on the pathway!' He agitated his little stout legs as he dangled them, as though he were already running for the border of the land to protect the little traveller from the Sprites.

Hedgehog the Traveller

Old Stripe nodded seriously. 'We shall tell Woo about this, as soon as he gets back. Then we'll think of a way to bring Old Candles safely to our houses.'

Mole's legs stopped their swinging, for he found it better to do one thing at a time; and for the moment he wanted to devote his full attention to the problem of the Hedgehog's coming.

Potter-the-Otter frowned over his pipe, ignoring the slow feeling of greed that was developing in his middle. He had higher thoughts to deal with.

While the folk waited in Owl's Beech, their departed host was rousing the Woodland with his friends of the air. Deep below the secret shadows of a copse, a Mole awoke, snug in his bedroom below the ground, and blinked in puzzlement as something came scuffling down his chimney. When he got up and lit a candle to see what was about, he found a big round stone, covered in soot, and a sooty piece of parchment to match.

Far away, over Silver-Birch Hill, a Rabbit was startled as a stone rattled into his hearth, and he ran to the window wondering what the soft rushing of wings could mean, so late at night.

High among the boughs of Marten's Elm, nearby the banks of the Wild River, a Pine-Marten, sleeping fitfully, was roused fully as a stone clanged sharply against the poker in the fireplace; and long before the Jackdaw who had dropped it was rising into the starlight, the Marten was peering at the urgent message from Owl's Beech.

In copse, in spinney, in the topmost branches of the highest trees, in large burrows and in small nests, everywhere in the Wood there woke the Woodlanders; and from their windows gleamed the light of single candles as they sought to discover the reason for the disturbance in their chimneys.

A Mole cried: 'The Goblins!' and made for his store-room to fetch a stout walking-stick.

A Hare gasped: 'Bolt the doors!'

A Badger cried: 'Bar the windows!'

An Otter called out—'Let's see a sign of 'em, and we'll give 'em Goblins!' and dashed to his front door to scan the riverside for the invaders, a long boat-hook in his angry old paw.

The Wood was waking, was warned, was ready. From a tall elm tree, a Jackdaw flew to Owl's Beech, after delivering his last message of alarm. From the spinneys beyond the Wild River two Magpies sped, swift-winged, striking through the shadows for the beech. From glen and glade came the birds, swooping homeward, their task done. With them came Owl, silent and shadowy, alighting on the window-sill of his private study, where his coming was awaited.

'What's a-going on in the Wood?' asked Old Stripe, when Woo was safely indoors. He brushed down his feathers and washed his wing-tips, which were sooty, and came importantly back to the study. The table was already spread with a small feast, for Scruff and Skip Squirrel—who both knew a mushroom from a clove—had been busy in the kitchen. It would be several hours yet before dawn broke; and there was still much to be done.

'Oh,' said Woo, relaxing gratefully into his largest arm-chair, 'there's plenty going on in the Wood, Old Stripe.' He blinked solemnly in the cheerful candle-light, for his eyes were still not quite accustomed to it after the dark-shadowed pathways through the leaves. 'Some of us saw the Hobgoblins, several times. And they saw *me*, once . . . '

Skip Squirrel gasped, and a blob of buttermilk fell by mistake into Old Stripe's pot of ale, as the small brown folk jerked his tufty head to look at Owl.

'What did they do?' he asked breathlessly.

Woo shrugged his well-padded shoulders and said casually, 'oh, they gave chase, you know—but they can't fly very fast, it seems. I outstripped 'em and went into a wide circle—' and he gestured with a large wing, so that Mole-the-Miller had to duck and dipped his long pink nose into a dish of cream— 'and turned back in my tracks to shadow them for a bit. I don't believe they've any proper wings, but they certainly carry blue lanterns with them by night. I heard them chattering and singing as they flew over Otter's Island—'

'Over *my* Island?' said Potter indignantly, and gripped his fork as though it were suddenly a weapon.

'They were round Badger's Beech, too,' nodded Owl, 'I heard them banging the knocker and howling down the chimneys.'

Old Stripe gave a shiver.

'Then I'm glad I wasn't in,' he said slowly. 'I never could bear loud noises and fuss and suchlike.'

He had just finished speaking when everyfolk was startled by a sudden chorus of strange voices. Potter leapt to his feet and dashed to the sitting-room crying 'Stand by for the attack!' while Old Stripe dropped his knife and fork with a clatter just as Scruff Fox darted for the back door and Mole-the-Miller ran from window to window, trying to sight the foe.

It had taken but a moment for the feast to break up; Woo Owl was wandering deedily about under the stairs, searching out his Ancient and Learned Books, to see if there were anything in them about How to Repel an Attack by Hobgoblins.

Mole-the-Miller, with the elfin chanting of the Sprites singing in his ears, now saw their mazy lanterns as they dived from the dark cloisters of the boughs and circled the beech with frenzied shouts of their squeaky voices.

'The beech is surrounded!' called Mole above the din; and he scampered all the way up the stairs to the highest landing of all to obtain a better view. Even now there sounded the mischievous knocking on the front door; and Scruff Fox, ready at his post round at the back, opened the door with a sudden flourish of fury and half a dozen blue lamps went whirling away in their fright.

'Ha!' cried the old Fox, shaking his paw into the night, 'I'll give ye Hobgobblies! Come a bit closer, why don't ye?'

But they came no closer. For many minutes they surrounded the great beech trees, drumming with mischievous fingers on the windows, hammering with small fists at the doors, chanting with eerie cadences down the chimneys. Old Stripe and Potter were more than ready for a real attack; yet none came. Scruff Fox nearly fell from the back door-step in his attempts to get to grips with the little Gnomes; Skip Squirrel and the Miller ran from place to place, guarding every entrance in turn, while Woo Owl thumbed the ancient pages of his learned Books, calling occasionally such remarks as—'Put salt on their tails! Creep up behind them! Cover their nests with treacle!'

But of course he was reading from the wrong pages, and soon gave it up. He climbed the stairs to the topmost landing, where Mole was hanging out of a half-open window, throwing acorns into the midst of the foe, and stood blinking largely on the amazing scene, trying to think what next to do.

Hedgehog the Traveller

He was annoyed, was Woo the Owl of Owl's Beech. His house was a dignified timber, and unused to such goings-on. His front door was intended to be opened, closed, and knocked upon gently by Callers and Visitors and Guests and Other Important People—not to be hammered at by irresponsibles.

It was when Woo Owl was gazing deedily from the topmost casement of his beech tree, wondering how best he might send these knaves packing, that he glimpsed another tiny lantern, far in the distance.

It was not blue, but winked with a yellow gleam. Now and then it was lost among the tree-boles, and then appeared again, to shine more brightly as minute followed upon minute. At first the Owl thought it must be the lamp of some Woodlander's homestead; then he wondered if it were a folk coming to the beech with a message; then he knew he was wrong in both theories, for this lantern was moving, and it was well beyond the borders of the Wood.

At last he knew whose lamp it must be, moving nearer the trees from the hills beyond. It was a traveller.

'Mole!' he said softly, 'you see that lantern, over in the distance?'

Mole stopped hurling acorns into the circling lights of the Hobgoblins, and drew his head inside. When he gazed at the fitful gleam of yellow light, he

knew instantly whose it must be. He turned to Owl
with a gasp:

'It's Candles the Hedgehog! Coming to the
Wood!'

Woo nodded slowly, thinking things out. This
required a steady head, for if the Gnomes caught
sight of the little traveller first, they'd be off to set
about him—and he'd have no friend to help him.

'Don't tell anyfolk, Mole,' he said suddenly.
'I'm going off to meet him! Try to draw the Gnomes
round to the other side of the tree, and I'll take off
from this window—'

He did not finish. Mole, looking down at the
Goblins, had seen them suddenly gathering in a
chattering throng; and now they were darting from
the tree, stringing their train of lamps across Woo's
Glade, and rising for the poplars on the far side.

'Woo!' cried Mole—'they've seen him! They've
seen Candles—'

The Owl said nothing in reply; Mole felt the
sudden rush of wings as the bird hopped to the
window, clambered upon the sill, poised there for
an instant, and then dived, his great wings spreading
and then beating into the darkness. Even as Mole
raced down the spiral staircase, he heard Woo's
voice booming among the trees to the Jackdaws
and Magpies and Woodpeckers—

'To the rescue! Woodlanders ahoy! Follow me,
follow me!'

His words faded in Mole's ears as he began shouting himself:

'Old Stripe! Potter! Scruff Fox!'

They met him in the hall, their eyes wide with amazement; for they had not seen the gleam of lantern-light from their positions lower in the tree.

'Candles is coming!' panted Mole, tugging at the front door-handle—'and the Gnomes have seen him!'

Like Woo Owl, they said nothing in reply. Mole had the door open and was clambering down the ladder with his short legs twinkling and his big pink paws slipping over the rungs as Old Stripe swung down after him, with Skip Squirrel treading on his stripey old head and Scruff Fox treading on Skip Squirrel's ears and Potter struggling to reach the ground in front of everyfolk else.

Their feet scampered across the starlit moss with the sound almost of small drum-beats as they dashed for the woodland pathway leading to Silver-Birch Hill. From the elms came Jackdaws and Rooks, diving down from their high dwellings and veering with dark and vengeful wings for the small gleam of lamplight that was still moving nearer from the hills.

A Raven, standing on guard at his doorstep, high on the South side of the Wood near Heather Hill, saw in the distance the skein of azure lamps that was the flight of Goblins. Behind them flew a dark shadow that was Owl, speeding to outstrip them; and after Owl were convoys of Rooks and Magpies, Jackdaws and Jays, their wings driving them onwards to the rescue of the lone traveller. And as the Raven dipped in an instant to join the chase, realising what it must mean, he saw the ground below him teeming with the shadowy shapes of Hares and Badgers, Moles and Weasels, Stouts and Squirrels, as the word went round—

'To the rescue! Rally the Woodlanders!'

Few of them knew whom they were to rescue;

few knew what the danger was. But most of them guessed: they had only just received the Owl's warning down their chimneys; and they remembered that soon the old Hedgehog must come with his barrow of candles.

Somewhere, far into the night, the little traveller stopped in the shadow of a copse, and peered into the trees. The Wood was usually wrapped in silence

and in sleep at this time of a night; and he had been thinking of snuggling beneath some dry and sheltered bank, to wait until morning. But now he was disturbed as he watched the skies.

High over the Wood there flew a skein of strange blue lamps, and the dark shapes of birds dotted the starfields behind. In the Hedgehog's sharp little ears there was the distant sound of many voices, and the pattering of many small feet.

The Wood was awake and abroad; and he wondered why.

His small bright lantern glowed above his barrow as he waited with a wrinkled brow, as nearer him and nearer him there came the strange blue hosts of the Hobgoblins, chanting eerily above the darkling wood.

Chapter 6

Fire at Full Moon

THE little Hedgehog, surrounded by his friends of the Wood, glanced up at the Hobgoblins who circled above them as they made their way through the spinneys. Old Stripe was talking to Candles, telling him the story of the blue lights; Skip Squirrel was pushing the barrow of candles while Potter-the-Otter tried to push it too; and most of the other folk—and there must have been fully half a hundred of them—kept as close as they could, in case the Gnomes decided to swoop down. Many folk carried a stick or a staff, and occasionally they brandished them at the stars, where the blue lamps drifted, chattering in chagrin.

If ever a folk had been offered safe conduct through the Wood, then the little traveller was receiving it now. The trees were loud with the murmur of the Hares and Badgers and Rabbits and Moles and their score of neighbours and friends; while above them flew the birds, circling and hovering, a constant guard for their fellow-woodlanders below. Now and then a bird would rise on swift wings to challenge the Hobgoblins, but without avail. Either the blue lamps would go scattering into the shelter of the leaves, or their light would vanish altogether, and only their elfin voices would remain.

Dawn was not far away from the skies above the Valley of Sweethallow, to the east of the Wood, when Candles and his friends reached Woo's Glade. And by the time he had thanked them all for their kindness, and had been taken up to Owl's big sitting-room, where there was a comfy chair awaiting him, the first pale glow of the new day was spreading on the far horizons, and touched the tops of the pines and cedars as though they were frosted under starlight.

'Well well,' said the candle-seller, as he sank gratefully into a chair, 'things have certainly changed in the Wood since I was here in the spring.' He looked comfortably round the big room, seeing the candle-light shining on the rich polished beechwood of the walls. Owl's house occupied about half the height of the great timber, and almost every room was round, with a staircase running upwards (or downwards, according to where a folk was a-going) against the wall. So it was rather like a light-house.

'I'm very sorry there was all this sort of fuss going on,' spoke up Old Stripe, 'just when you came to see us again. But there was nothing we could do about it.'

Hedgehog nodded slowly, his small bright eyes moving to watch the faces of his good friends. He loved them well, and one day would come to Deep Wood to live among them, as once he had done before. Two years he had been a Woodlander, content to dwell in Old Stripe's quiet house, until the call of the pathways came to him again; and off he had gone, trundling a special new barrow made for him by old Mr. Nibble of Deep Wood Store. Some day, he had promised them, he'd return for all time; but for the present the pathways of the world drew him beyond the hills and across the oceans of the earth.

'Fuss, Old Stripe,' he said, answering the Badger, 'and bother, yes. But as you say, you couldn't help it.'

He spoke in a dreamy voice, and his eyes were fixed with a deep and secret expression on the mantelpiece, where stood two candles burning, their light struggling to combat the first few sunbeams that were slanting now through the trees. Old Stripe watched the Hedgehog in silence. It was quite clear that the old traveller was thinking of something else—maybe something thousands of miles away from this green land.

'Fuss,' murmured the candle-maker, 'and bother yes . . . ' and he looked up at the Badger. 'Ah,' he added. 'I was just thinking, you know, about Gnomes and such folk. It's very queer.'

94

'Too queer,' grunted Potter-the-Otter. 'It's high time they stopped making a nuisance of themselves in the Wood.'

Hedgehog nodded slowly, and said: 'High time, my dear Potter indeed. But the question in my mind is *why did they begin?*'

'They began,' said Skip Squirrel, 'in Sweethallow Valley, before they came on the Wind to the Wood.'

'And why did they begin in the Valley?' persisted Old Candles. 'Why should they begin *anywhere?*'

But no-folk knew the answer. Only Old Stripe, who was perhaps closer to the little traveller than any other, knew that behind his seemingly trivial question there must lie a good reason.

'What are you thinking?' he asked the Hedgehog quietly, as he drew on his black briar pipe.

'Thinking?' said Hedgehog slowly, 'why, I'm thinking just what I've told you. There must be a *reason* for these Sprites to visit the Wood—or to visit anywhere outside their own Erldom. And it might be interesting to discover.'

'Go on,' murmured the Badger, knowing his prickly friend wanted drawing out. 'What do you know of these strange folk?'

'Oh, I've seen them, many a time,' said the traveller. 'But only when I've been passing near their own lands. They keep to Ireland, mostly, where they're known as the little People. But I've never seen them so far afield as this. And it sets me wondering.'

Though Old Stripe tried again to make the little fellow say more of what he knew about the Hob-goblins, he seemed to want the quiet contemplation of his own deep thoughts, while he sat smoking of his little brown corn-cob pipe. So finally they stopped their questions, and Owl showed them where there was a snug bedroom for each of them in his tall old house.

The Hedgehog stayed for a moment, talking softly to Old Stripe and Woo as they finished their pipes; but he did not refer to the Goblins again that night—or rather, that morning, for dawn had now broken and the wood was drenched in pale sunshine.

The sun was high overhead when the folk in Owl's Beech woke at last. Woo Owl was first in the kitchen, and was just putting the kettle on when Stripe came wandering down the spiral staircase.

'Ah,' said Woo largely, his eyes blinking slowly as he waited for his feathery old brain to wake up properly.

'Good morning, Woo, old chap,' said the Badger, 'or good afternoon, or something. Are we the first downstairs?'

'I am,' nodded Woo gently, working out the problem of whether to stand the kettle with the spout pointing *away* from the chimney or *towards* it.

'But you're not,' he added, by way of early-morning conversation.

'Oh,' said Stripe, slightly disappointed. He wandered carefully over to the kitchen range, and watched Woo trying to kindle a flame with his tinder-box. Old Woo always took rather a long time to wake up properly, first thing of a Summer's morning, as did Old Stripe and Old Potter and the rest of them. They never hurried, for it gave them indigestion and wind and palsies and such. Waking-up had to be a nice slow, deedy, cautious sort of affair.

'There . . . ' mumbled Stripe contentedly, as Woo managed at last to get the fire crackling. He wandered carefully over to the cupboard where the coffee was kept.

'I wonder,' said Woo, as they sat comfortably in the first sunbeams that slanted through the east window of the room, 'what Old Candles was thinking about, last night, when he said there must be a *reason* for the Hobgoblins being here in the Wood.'

'Ah,' said Stripe, and took some more sugar for his cup. 'He knows a lot about a lot of things, does Hedgehog. He might even know how we can get rid of the Gobblies. I wonder where they are this morning?'

A large, dark-blue plume of smoke burst suddenly from the stove and rolled silently into the room, thick and curdled in the sunbeams. Woo leapt to his feet and opened a window, while Stripe went into a high old coughing-fit that took him twice round the room and by complete surprise. After everything had settled down, Woo blinked mildly:

'Still about, it seems.' He fanned his wings up and down to clear the air thoroughly, turned to glare gently at his fire, and returned to the table to finish his cup of coffee. He was just about to make further remarks on the subject of Hobgoblins and their nasty little tricks, when there was a soft tapping on the door.

'Come in!' boomed Owl, grasping a large wooden spoon, just in case.

Candles the Hedgehog peeped through the doorway. Woo put his spoon down, and got up.

'You're just in time for a little something, my dear Hedgefolk. Come and sit down, and we'll look in my pantry.'

Hedgefolk stood blinking his small bright eyes in puzzlement for a while.

'Has—has something been catching fire?' he enquired.

Old Stripe, gazing dreamily into the pantry, searched round in his fur to see if he'd tucked his pipe away somewhere while it was still burning.

'Not me, this time,' he said innocently (for it usually was when there was a smell of burning).

Woo indicated the fire, with an indignant sweep of

his wing. 'It's the Goblins again,' he told Hedgehog.

Old Stripe stopped fumbling for possible warm pipes, and said, 'There you are, then,' and went back to looking in Woo's pantry.

'The Goblins . . . ' murmured Candles, and sat down on the window-seat, watching Woo while he made some more coffee. 'What have they been doing now?'

'Blowing down me chimney,' grunted Woo, wishing they wouldn't. 'You just wait till I catch one!'

'How are you going to do that?' asked Hedgehog simply.

'We don't know, but we shall, somehow.'

'There is a way, and a very simple one.'

Woo stopped stirring coffee, and looked at the candle-maker. Old Stripe stopped looking at rows of jam-pots and jars of marmalade, and looked at Hedgehog instead.

'Oh?' they said. He nodded.

'But I fear I don't quite remember it.'

Old Stripe's gaze wandered back to the collection of jam and marmalade on the pantry shelf.

'Then we don't seem to be much better off, do we?' he asked a large and imposing pot of honey.

Woo Owl was stirring coffee again.

'We don't,' he said, not looking at Hedgehog either. Old Hedgehog was usually such a sensible little folk.

99

'Yes,' repeated Candles gently, 'there *is* a way, certainly—'

'And a very simple one,' nodded Old Stripe patiently from the cupboard.

'But we don't quite remember what,' agreed Woo heavily, adding a dash of cold water to settle the coffee-grounds.

'I don't remember *what*,' admitted Hedgehog, 'but I *do* remember where I read about it.'

Old Stripe didn't look round from the cupboard. He'd heard that sort of thing before. Woo Owl poured out three rich cups of golden-coloured coffee, added a generous clot of cowslip-cream to each, and said:

'Where?'

'In your Ancient and Learned Books,' murmured Hedgehog, and scratched the tip of his pointed nose in a remembering kind of way. After Old Stripe had stopped inspecting the lemon-curd, and Woo had stopped making more coffee to be going on with, the candle-maker nodded vigorously. 'That's where I read about it,' he said with conviction.

So it was that when Skip Squirrel and Potter-the-Otter came down to see what was being done about breakfast, now that folk were up and about and very hungry, they found Woo and Stripe and Candles busily poring over three immense volumes on the kitchen table.

So huge were these three particular Learned

Books that they combined to cover the entire table, and Stripe was reading Page One of Volume Two round and round a dish of cream, while Woo kept moving his cup of coffee to-and-fro as he read Page Four of Volume Three. Hedgehog was at this

moment trying to turn his page over, but there seemed nowhere to put the coffee-pot and plate of muffins that were holding it down at present.

'Top o' the morning!' called Skip cheerfully, rubbing his hands and peering at folk.

'Sorry we're late,' added Potter (who was seldom given to being late for breakfast—or any other meal).

They blinked expectantly at their large and usually dutiful host, Woo Owl, and at his two friends. There was a decidedly pleasant aroma of coffee in the room; and there was a kettle on the hob, a-going dancing with its lid for all the world as though it were boiling. The stage, indeed, appeared to be well set for a large and comfortable breakfast. Potter and Skip blinked even more expectantly, noting this.

But the three folk continued to pore over their large and apparently absorbing books. Skip gave Potter a nudge.

'Thinking up a Special Recipe,' he whispered, 'for a Hextra-Special Breakfast.' Potter nodded cheerfully; and they sat down on the window-seat, stroking their middles to let them know what was about.

'Take ye gizzard of an elder-flower,' boomed Woo of a sudden, reading from his book. He glanced up. 'What d'you make of that, Old Stripe?'

Old Stripe placed his paw carefully on the spot where he was reading, so it shouldn't go off while he wasn't looking, and said:

'Do they have them?'

'Do they have what?' asked Candles, glancing up.

'Do *what* have what?' enquired Woo.

Skip Squirrel turned his head and looked at Potter. Potter shook his head. He didn't quite follow all this.

'Do elder-flowers have gizzards, is what I mean,' said Old Stripe.

Woo returned to his book. 'I'm not sure. But it says here: "Take ye gizzard of an elder-flower, and mix with ye hearts of twain deadly-nightshade. Heat over ye flame of a blazing brand, then sprinkle ye juices o'er the land." You see?'

Old Stripe did not. Woo looked at Hedgehog. Hedgehog said:

'Um'mm.'

'Well there you are,' said Woo, rather wishing some folk would become more enthusiastic on this Goblin-Remedy he'd found in his Learned Book.

Potter-the-Otter, sitting quietly with Skip Squirrel on the window-seat, patted his middle in puzzlement. Here were their three good friends, apparently working out a recipe for a Special Breakfast, yet there seemed to be some little error.

'I always say there's nothing like a bit of toast and marmalade,' murmured Skip Squirrel, by way of helping.

Woo Owl glanced behind him.

'That won't do it,' he complained. And just as he was about to glance in front of him instead of behind him, he looked back and said: 'Well, well, well—hello Skip! When did you arrive?'

'Before breakfast,' said Potter pointedly. Skip nodded.

'Before *breakfast*,' he said. They sat quietly again.

'Deadly nightshade seems the right sort of thing, I must say,' they heard Old Stripe.

'Not this morning, thank you,' said Skip, with a worried look at his friend Potter.

'Please help yourselves to something snacky, would you?' said Woo Owl absent-mindedly to his newly-arrived guests. 'I think there's plenty in the cupboard, and the kettle's boiling.'

He returned to his chapter headed: 'How to Rid ye Land of ye Horrid Hobgoblin.'

'Try some Dragon's-breath and brimstone,' murmured Old Stripe, reading round his butter-knife.

Potter glanced at Skip, and wandered firmly towards the pantry. He knew Woo's pantry of old, and he was quite sure they could squeeze a goodly breakfast from it without trying Dragon's-nightshade, or whatever these absurd folk were talking about.

'It seems to me,' said Hedgehog, managing to turn over another page by balancing his plate on Old Stripe's head for a moment, 'that we shall have to follow the instructions I've found here. I think this is the simple way I remember reading about.'

'Ah,' said Woo Owl, and fixed his small and prickly friend with an attentive stare. Old Stripe stopped trying to spread some more butter by mistake on Paragraph Three of Page Six, and prepared himself to listen.

'How does it go?' he asked the candle-seller.

Hedgehog read slowly from his enormous book:

' "Wait until ye Moon is fulle, then burn upon a pyre ye sprigs of Lavender, as many as is found within a day's search. For ye Horid Sprites and Elves are enamoured of such a smell." '

Hedgehog sat back, and waited for their comment.

In the silence, the only murmur came from Potter, speaking from the shelter of Woo's large pantry:

'Pity. I suppose it's the hot weather or something.'

'I think the real trouble,' replied Skip, munching a jam-tart to himself, 'is that they haven't woken up properly yet. We'll give them a call in a moment. Would you care for some lemon-curd on that strawberry flan, old chap?'

Woo Owl and Old Stripe and Candles the Hedgehog frowned slightly, hearing these absurd and meaningless interruptions. Theirs was serious business, and all folk could think of talking about was lemon-curd . . .

'Wait until ye moon is full,' said Stripe reflectively. 'And how long is that going to take?'

Potter glanced at Skip in the pantry.

'We were both wrong, after all. It's the full moon that's troubling them—you just listen.'

'Now let me see,' said Woo, gazing deedily at the ceiling, where a spider was breakfasting upon a morsel of cake he'd just been down to the table to fetch. 'Today is a Tuesday, I believe. That means yesterday was—erm—'

'Tomorrow,' complained Stripe, 'is what we want. Because it's the *next* full moon we're after, not the *last*.'

Potter looked at Skip.

'There you are,' he said, nodding seriously.

'Tomorrow, then, must be on a Wednesday,' said Woo, thinking it peculiar that spiders should like currant cake.

'And it's a new moon tonight,' said Stripe, who always watched his almanack closely at Badger's Beech.

'Ah,' said Hedgehog. 'Then there'll be a full one in about six nights.'

Woo nodded, as an accidental cake-crumb came down onto his left ear from the web on the ceiling.

'Then we'll gather all the lavender we can, and burn it in the Glade with the next full moon,' he said. 'That'll send them packing!'

'If what the Book says is right,' nodded Hedgehog.

'We'll try it,' Old Stripe murmured, and scraped a blob of apple-jelly off a picture of an Ancient Elfin in his massive volume. 'We'll go down to Lavender Copse this very day, and gather all we can.' He sat back contentedly, satisfied not only with an ample breakfast but with the thoughts that at last something was really being done about the Horrid

Hobgoblins. 'Now as soon as the others come down, we'll tell them what we've decided, and ask them to help. If they ever get down at all, the lazy things.'

Potter blinked at Skip, in the depths of the cupboard.

'Good-morning, Old Stripe,' he suggested mildly.

The Badger looked over his shoulder.

'Oh,' he said, 'so you're over there, are you? I might have known, of course.'

'I believe our good friends have been with us some little while,' said Woo hastily, and struggled to his feet. 'I remember asking them to help themselves to some breakfast, while we deliberated upon our problem, but it doesn't excuse me from acting as a proper host. Have you found sufficient, Potter old chap?'

'If I know anything of Potter-old-chap,' murmured Stripe, 'he will have found far more than sufficient.'

By the time Potter had waxed indignant and had helped himself to further delicacies from Woo's pantry, Scruff Fox and Mole-the-Miller came down, stroking their middles in that reflective way they always had about this time of day.

It was late afternoon when they were told of the plan to expel the Goblins from the Wood; and none of them protested at the idea. If Woo's Ancient and Learned Book said that burning lavender was the answer to the problem, then much would be burned and with a will.

That night, the new moon lifted from the horizon above Sweethallow Valley, and Old Stripe, who saw it first, nodded slowly. His almanack was right. In six nights it would be full and shining in the skies and they would make their pyre of lavender-sprigs. What the immediate result would prove to be, nobody knew for sure. Woo said 'enamoured' meant the Goblins would *like* the scent of the burning sprigs, and that the idea was to attract them to one spot, where they could be surrounded and trapped. So the Woodlanders were more than ready.

Between the Tuesday of the new moon and the Monday that followed, the Sprites made a nuisance of themselves in their usual ways. They blew down chimneys and sent smoke a-skirling into the rooms; they chanted by night, and mazed their blue-shining way among the sleeping trees. They knocked upon doors and tapped upon windows, snuffed a folk's candle and turned a folk's milk; and long before full-moon came, the people of Deep Wood were heartily tired of their tricks.

But Monday evening arrived at last.

It seemed, to anyfolk who didn't know, that Monday evening was as ordinary as always. Truly, there stood a huge pile of lavender-boughs in the very middle of Woo's Glade; but it was not burning and its scent was but faint in the twilight. Folk, before sunset, were in their homes, smoking a pipe after supper or telling a story while the stars came out, one by one above the tallest trees.

But, when the last shreds of gold had fled the skies to the West, and when the moon rose, huge and silver among the starry wastes, the Woodlanders moved, one by one like the lamps of the night, to their secret places in the trees.

At midnight, when the Goblins were drifting through a spinney close by Fox End, trying to annoy Scruff Fox by singing a raucous ditty, this very folk stole from the shadows of Owl's Beech, and struck a tinder beneath the pile of lavender sprigs in the middle of the moonlit Glade.

As soon as the flame licked the first branches, Scruff crept back to the tree, where Old Stripe stood with Potter, each with a stick in his paw.

To the eyes of a bird, happening to fly above the Wood at this late hour, the trees would have seemed asleep, and every Woodlander in his own snug bed. Yet he would have been deceived.

Many small bright eyes watched the slow fire that climbed the lavender-pile. In the elms sat a dozen Rooks, and with them a dozen Crows. In the deep crown of leaves held aloft by Owl's Beech there waited Woo himself, together with his friends the Jackdaws and the Woodpeckers. In every tree there were winged folk a-waiting, their feathers furled, their eyes watching the pyre below them in the Glade.

From the shadows of the lower trees, there watched the Squirrels and the Pine Martens, from their houses and from the crooks of gnarled boughs; each was armed with a stout stick, and some even had coils of cord, in case it was possible to lasso a Goblin as he flew past.

From the ground, beneath bush and shrub, from the gloom of burrow and of bank, there watched Badgers and Weasels, Otters and Voles, Stoats and Moles, each with two bright eyes unwinking, each with two sharp ears alert.

As the flames leapt crimson about the lavender, driving back the shadows and spilling scarlet over the moss, the eyes of the Woodlanders moved sometimes towards the frieze of trees, silhouetted against the starfields where the full moon sailed, silver and serene.

From the height of the great tree, Woo Owl whispered to a neighbour: 'I wonder if the book told us aright.'

Far below him, crouched in the shadows of the massive trunk, Old Stripe turned to Potter and murmured: 'I wonder if they'll come . . . '

From the banks and the burrows, from the tree-tops and the high turrets of the oaks, folk said: 'How long will they be?'

They were not long, the Goblins.

Fire at Full Moon

They came, the Goblins, as the flames of the
lavender leaped and danced alone within the
moonlit glade; as the boughs blazed, as the smoke
writhed, twisting with blue tendrils upwards to the
night-sky, they came, the Goblins, darting and
drifting from the northern reaches of Deep Wood.
their elfin laughter shrilling to the trees, their bright
blue lanterns mazing through the leaves, until—
until they circled the very flames of the burning
sprigs and danced around and sang aloud to the
chattering of the crackling embers.

The night was spread and decked with the colours
—silver of the watching moon, crimson of the
leaping flames, sapphire-blue of the wreathing
Gnomes, emerald of the lacing leaves that did not
move, not one of them, in the still night airs.

As they span and frolicked round the rising
flames, the Goblins laughed aloud and sang on high
to the moon; and as their voices reached to the
farthest copse, to the tallest tree on the distant hills,
the Owl on the height of the giant beech cried
'Now!'—and spread his wings.

Chapter 7

The Feast at Owl's Beech

WHEN the folk of the Woodland opened their midnight attack upon the Hobgoblins, they had been prepared for a sharp struggle, and an exchange of blows. Each Woodlander was armed with some kind of rough weapon; each carried determination in the beat of his swooping wings, in the stamp of his fleet foot over the moss.

But one of them held back. He was not strictly a Woodlander, for his name was Candles the Hedgehog. He stood now beneath the gnarled old trunk of Owl's Beech, just watching. The traveller, old though he was, could give a fair account of himself when there was trouble about and fur was flying; so he did not hold back at this moment for lack of courage. No, he was *waiting*.

Versed in the ways of woodland folk, he knew them. He knew almost as much of Goblins and their tricks, for he had passed by their lands many a time. And he knew, thirdly, that the Ancient and Learned Books in Woo Owl's study were brimmed with wisdom and sound counsel, for they had been writ by many an ancestor of Owl himself, centuries ago when much deep philosophy had been granted the folk of the land.

Therefore little old Hedgehog waited. The Book should be telling aright when it gave the burning of lavender as the means of ridding a place of the Horrid Hobgoblins. There had been no mention of fighting or trapping or chasing. Burn these sprigs by the light of a full moon, and wait.

Candles waited, his bright eyes gleaming from the shadow of the tree.

And he was right, even as the Book was right.

Before Woo Owl had swooped a dozen feet from the high bough of his beech, his wings curved vengefully, his eyes glaring at the blue-lit foe, an amazing thing happened. Before he shaped for the onslaught, and before his every friend, Bird, Fur-Folk, Burrow or Tree-Dweller, could join him against the Imps, their strange blue lamps went out so swiftly that it was as though a great gust of wind had snuffed them and was gone.

Watching the curious scene, little Hedgefolk held his breath. The fire of lavender was leaping still, curling its crimson tongues about the branches and throwing its roseate light around the pile so that the Glade might have been the depths of a huge rose-flower, so ruby were the encircling trees in the firelight.

As every bird came diving from the silver of the skies their wings flashed as though frosted by the moon, until they neared the ground, when the warm flush of the fireglow shone rufous upon their vaned pinions, and the silver-front was gone.

As every Fur-Folk came darting from the shadows, their feet stamping over the moss with sound of drum-fire, their coats were tinged with the crimson light, and it seemed as though an army of scarlet-breasted soldiers were driving from the trees, each one closing towards the centre, each determined to reach the foe before his fellows.

But the foe was vanquished, already. The blue lights were gone, so swiftly that their sapphire gleams seemed still to drift and circle near the burning pyre. From each lantern now there floated downwards a single form—and seeing them, the Woodlanders held back, amazed.

With a flurry of straining wings, the birds diverted their downward rush, and landed swiftly on the mossy floor, even as the racing Fur-Folk pulled up sharply, tumbling over one another as the birds came down among them. Within an instant they had formed a great circle about the leaping fire; and within their ring there fell these strange shapes that once had been lamps of blue.

As the Gnomes came down, sprawling and

struggling on the ground, the flames of the fire began dying slowly, as though they were aware that the task was done. But their ruby light was still as bright as a harvester's moon; and gradually the Woodlanders saw the mysterious forms of the Goblins assume a clear and definite outline before their astonished gaze.

There was no voice here in the Wood, not one. No sound was heard from the Goblins as they struggled to their feet and drew together, huddled and afraid. No Woodlander uttered a single word as they watched the strange secret of the Hobgoblins unfolding in the fireglow.

The only sound, above the low murmur of the lavender boughs, was the hurrying shuffle of two small feet, as little Hedgehog came quickly from Owl's Beech, and pressed his way through the throng of Woodlanders until he stood at last in front of the group of Gnomes, alone.

Potter-the-Otter, thinking they might attack the little prickle-folk, made to join him; but Old Stripe knowing how wise was Candles, drew the Otter back, with a quick shake of his head.

As though he recognized the Hedgehog as the spokesman of the Woodland people, a single Goblin came forward from his fellows, and, drawing up within a few feet of the candle-seller, bowed low to him. For a moment Hedgehog looked at him, remembering others he had seen upon his travels through distant Ireland. This was akin to those he had met before.

He was smaller even than the candle-maker, and barely half his height. Upon his head there sat a quaint and pointed cap of emerald cloth; and from his puckish face there dangled a silvery beard, down

to the middle button of the curious tunic of dark green that was belted about him. Breeches of the same leaf-colour he wore, and two bright shoes, buckled with pure gold.

Old Stripe and his many friends of the Wood had never seen such a folk as this; and they were silent as they watched the fascinating scene. They knew Hedgehog and his wisdom, and were content to let him carry off this curious situation as his judgement told him.

A deep twinkle lay in the candle-maker's eyes as he made to speak. He knew that with the going of the blue lanterns, the magic power of the Gnomes was no longer theirs to wield.

His voice reached clearly to every ear, though his words were for the Imps alone:

'Greetings to Deep Wood, my friends. We are glad to see you here.'

A swift and sudden murmur of surprise ran for a moment through the score of Goblins, and they looked to their leader in bewilderment.

His voice was as quaint as his dress; it bubbled as silver waters through glistening rocks, yet was as dry as tinderwood.

'You—you are glad to see us? Why?' And his small hands were spread out in puzzlement.

'Because you are travellers,' said Candles softly, 'just as I myself. And all travellers are welcome in the Wood.'

'Welcome?'

The word was repeated by the Gnome as though it had never passed his lips before.

Old Candles nodded slowly, the twinkle in his eyes deepening as he talked.

'Of course. In Deep Wood, a traveller is a visitor; and a visitor is a guest. Every door is open to him. Every hearth is ready to warm him. Every table is spread for his hunger, and every bed for his rest. Do you understand?'

The Hobgoblin clearly did not. He was here to make great nuisance with his friends; to sour the milk and to knock at the doors and to tap at the windows and to make the night loud with eerie chanting. He was here with them to dismay the folk who lived in the trees. Yet they were welcomed . . .

'We are from the land of the Erl King!' he said, thinking perhaps this quaint and prickly creature was not aware of it.

Hedgehog nodded calmly.

'A traveller is welcome whether he comes from the white wastes of the north or the sunshine of the south. He is an honoured guest, from China or Peru.' He turned and gestured with his paw to Old Stripe and Woo and Potter and their many friends. 'These are the folk of Deep Wood,' he told the Leprechaun. 'No matter to them *where* a folk *comes* from—he *is* in the *Wood*, and is welcome. You see?'

The Gnome frowned deeply, trying to puzzle this out. He was surely relieved to hear these amazing words, for he and his fellows had lost their magic in the smoke of lavender, and were powerless before these hosts of woodlanders. But he still could not understand why they were not already being bound in chains and thrown to deep dungeons for their trickery in the trees.

The Feast at Owl's Beech

Saying nothing to little Candles, he span upon his sprightly heel and went to talk in low whispers with the others. Hedgehog gave a chuckle, and turned to Old Stripe:

'They don't understand, Stripey, but we'll make them. Was I wrong in telling them? Are they really welcome in the Wood?'

Old Stripe puckered his black-and-white brows and nodded slowly, himself bewildered by the change in events.

'As welcome as any traveller, just as you said,' he told Candles. 'Well, Potter-the-Otter?'

Potter-the-Otter was looking at the group of Goblins less kindly. He was very fond of his water-wheel, was old Potter-Folk, for it had been built with his very own paws, and was the finest water-wheel in the lands about Deep Wood. But these rascally folk had played all manner of tricks and up-and-down with it, and he was still cross.

Even so, he was a Woodlander; and the Imps were guests—according to Hedgehog.

'I suppose they're welcome,' he said reluctantly. 'But there'll be no more nonsense and fiddle-faddle, if they want to warm themselves at *my* hearth.'

The other folk agreed with him. The Gnomes could stay as guests—if they behaved as such.

'And by way of proving our word,' said Woo Owl to little Hedgehog, 'please allow me to offer my immediate hospitality.'

'So you shall,' nodded the candle-maker.

Woo puffed up his chest-feathers so high and puffy that he could scarcely see where he was going as he advanced with stately gait across the Glade. The Goblins ceased chattering together as they saw him approach.

'My dear—erm—Friends,' began Woo, in the special boom-tone he adopted when receiving guests and such folk. 'I am happy to—erm—offer you my hosp—hospi—'

'—tility,' suggested Potter from behind him.

'My hospitality,' boomed Woo, 'exactly. So if you will be kind enough to follow me, we shall proclaim a feast—'

But at this last word, there came a scuffling sound from Potter as he struggled through the throng and dashed for Woo's visiting-ladder. He was first on the doorstep when Stripe and Mole-the-Miller came puffing and panting up to the porch, to help the Owl usher his quaint little guests inside.

'Potter,' murmured Stripe below the general conversation, 'would you mind seeing to the chairs?'

'Seeing to them, Stripey?' asked Potter, hoping to give Woo enough time to ask him to help in the kitchen instead.

'Well there'll be a house-full,' pointed out the Badger.

'Oh, exactly.' Potter ambled off reluctantly, and Skip Squirrel went with him to help sort out as many chairs as could be found in Woo's rambling old house.

Though midnight was well gone, it was decided to hold a feast of welcome there and then; and long before the moon was riding lower beyond the Western hills, a high old party was a-going on in and around the great beech tree. There were folk in the dining-room, the drawing-room, the morning-room; there were tables on the moss in the moonlit glade, decked with candle-light and flagons of ancient ale.

The Jackdaws and Woodpeckers, Jays and Magpies flew to their neighbouring houses and back again, bringing many a delicacy for the feast. Other folk went off to their nearby dwellings, to return with a few more flagons of rich cherry-wine, or another jar of baccy for their pipes.

By dawn the merry-making was at its height. The tables, that before had sagged to dishes of chestnut-pies, mushroom-puddings, roasted potatoes and walnut-stuffing, were now bright with bowls of fruit—apples, new-garnered from the store-rooms; pears and peaches, plums and strawberries—and dish upon dish there was of honey flans and chocolate cake, cowslip cream and cloverdew, until the twenty Hobgoblins were quiet with amaze at the overwhelming hospitality of Woo and the Wood-landers.

Many a folk was still sipping at his wine when the

E

sun came up, and most of them were drawing on their new-lit pipes. Old Stripe was striking up a sprightly tune on his one-stringed fiddle, and Skip was piping with him on a flute. Scruff Fox was singing a Ballad of the Wood in his deepest baritone, sitting astride a bough above the front door, and a

dozen Rabbits from South Burrow were dancing a Rabbit Reel across the soft green moss of the glade.

Woo Owl was making sure his especial guests were plied with every delicacy and offered the choicest blends of baccy from the Badger's own workshop in the Beech. As yet, the Gnomes boasted not a smoking-pipe among them; but they used lengths of reed-stem, plucked from the banks of the

Wild River, until Stripe—as he promised—had time to make a score of briars for them in his snug pipe-making room at home.

As the sun warmed the feast, drenching the Glade with its strengthening beams toward mid-morning, folk began drifting to their own homes, half-asleep on their small furry feet, and quite bewildered with the wine. Woo Owl threw open his many spare bedrooms, but several guests chose to curl up on the soft-warm moss, to close their eyes and wrap their tails about their ears, while their whiskers went a-trembling to their snores.

The happiest folk among the whole woodland company was perhaps little old Hedgehog. He had known there was a way to break the spell of the Goblins; and he had hoped that, once the magic was lost to them, they would prove to be good friends and welcome guests in the trees. They had spoken little during the feasting, for they still seemed too amazed at their reception; and still dazed, maybe, by the breaking of their powers upon the fire of lavender.

They might prove yet to be mischievous folk; but the candle-seller bided his time, for time would tell him.

'Well, old Candles,' said Stripe to him, as they stood talking over a last pipe in a quiet corner, 'I've seen some times in the Wood, but none like these!'

The Feast at Owl's Beech

'I'm glad I was here, Old Stripe,' chuckled Hedgehog contentedly. 'We don't know the real measure of these queer little people yet, but with a little encouragement and a bit of honest friendship, they might make goodly neighbours. I'm still looking forward to a long talk with them, and I'm going to ask them how they came to leave their own lands. Usually they keep themselves to themselves, you know.'

Old Stripe glanced at his friend of the pathways, sensing the quiet excitement of his tone.

'You still think there's a reason for their being here, Candles?' he murmured.

'There's reason,' said he, 'for everything.'

By and by, the Hedgehog stole away to a cosy spare-room in Owl's Beech, to take himself to bed and to wonder a few minutes more on the coming of the Hobgoblins to the Wood.

The Badger wandered through the drawing-room and through the hall and out onto the wide front porch, where Mole-the-Miller was finishing his little black pipe before curling up just where was handiest to sleep.

'Well, Moley,' sighed Old Stripe, sitting down and making himself comfortable in the warm sunshine, 'what d'ye think of this little turn of events?'

'I'm blessed if I know,' said Mole, leaning gently on Stripe's furry shoulder and closing his eyes. 'But I think there's a folk who does.'

'Old Hedgehog,' nodded Stripe sleepily, watching the smoke from his pipe drifting into the sunlit air. '*He* knows.'

'He knows, all right . . . ' murmured Mole-the-Miller; and before the Badger could say more to him, his small pink nose was wrinkled in the beginning of a Mole-snore, and his big pink paws were folded comfortably over his taut velvet middle, and the toes of his left foot wriggled suddenly in delight as they felt a dream coming on.

Old Stripe leaned harder on Mole, to balance them better, and his cherrywood pipe drooped lower and lower until it rested on his chest; and the last skein of blue smoke went drifting dreamily into the sunshine that filtered through the beech leaves. Somewhere a Bird called, far across the hills; and somewhere a leaf stirred on the bough above them.

And somewhere, deep in his dreams, the Badger murmured softly—'he knows, all right . . . '

Meaning Hedgehog.

Chapter 8

The Badger's Dream

POTTER-THE-OTTER was gliding down the Wild River in his little blue boat, *Bunty*; and with him was Skip Squirrel. Neither of them was using the oars, for the current was slow and comfortable, and they had until evening to reach the point nearest to Fallen Elm, the Squirrel's house near the river-bank. At this moment Skip wasn't saying nuffin; and all Potter was saying was a sort of 'fuff-fuff-fuff' as his occasional snore played an occasional tune on his quivering whiskers. Potter had had lunch; and now he was dreaming about it, very gently, until Skip said:

'Are you asleep, Potter-the-Otter?'

'Yes,' replied he, without hesitation. Skip regarded him.

'How d'you know?' he asked interestedly. There was no-folk like old Potter for eating and sleeping; and the small bushy-tailed folk wanted to know how it was done.

Potter-the-Otter opened his left eye, which would be sufficient to show him all he wanted to see just now, and observed his small and fidgety friend, lying back comfortably in the bows.

'I knew I was asleep,' he explained patiently, 'because I have just been Woken Up. Therefore I must have been asleep. It's all very simple.'

'Ah,' murmured Skip, and looked up at the deep blue sky. 'It's a nice afternoon,' he suggested cosily. He watched the great white ships of cumulus sailing across the blue, and nodded at them contentedly.

Potter opened his right eye and saw his friend Skip Squirrel twice as clearly.

'An exceeding nice afternoon,' he grunted. 'And now that we've decided upon that being so, and such, perhaps no-folk might object if I went to sleep again.'

'Am I disturbing you?' asked Squirrel.

'Disturbing me?' Potter slipped gently backwards on the cushions so that his taut and furry middle should be more exposed to the sunshine, for it was a goodly thing to be a-doing. 'Disturbing me?' he said again, 'oh, no. By no means, my dear Skip. I *like* talking in my sleep.'

Skip watched him as his eyes closed again, and something remarkably snore-like worked its way through his shiny whiskers.

'Are you really talking in your sleep?' enquired Squirrel in surprise (for the subject always interested him).

'Trying to,' murmured Potter pointedly.

'Is it very difficult?' Skip wanted to know.

'I have never realised,' replied Potter carefully, 'just *how* difficult it is—until now.'

Skip worked all this out in his small furry mind, and was just about to enquire further upon this highly interesting matter when a movement attracted his attention.

'Potter,' he said cheerfully.

Potter said nothing. There were some folk who just didn't appreciate what it meant to go to sleep on a nice well-filled tum. There were some folk who just didn't realise what it meant to—

'Potter-the-Otter!'

Potter-the-Otter opened his eyes, struggled on his cushion until he was sitting almost upright, regarded the river with an expression of extreme patience, regarded the small brown folk who sat before him, and said slowly:

'It certainly is.'

Skip blinked at him.

'Certainly is what?' he enquired.

'A nice afternoon,' said Potter heavily. 'Isn't that what you were going to ask me again? Well it is. Very nice. So quiet, and peaceful, isn't it? Just the sort of afternoon that makes a folk want to curl up somewhere and have a snooze. I've always said the best thing in the world, except of course for having a large and comfortable lunch, is having a short and comfortable snooze. Especially just *after* a large and com—'

'Potter,' broke in Skip Squirrel, 'there's a folk.'

Potter looked at him.

'What sort?' he said, in case it were.

'One like me.' Skip waved a small paw in the direction of the East bank of the river. 'Brown and furry and with tufts on his ears.'

Potter gave a sigh.

'That,' he pointed out patiently, 'is your reflection. Water is funny that way. You look at it, and suddenly you find there's two of you.' He added quietly, under his Otter-breath: 'and that is exactly twice as disturbing.'

'No,' persisted Skip—'over there, on the bank.'

His friend gazed over the ripples to the bank, and saw, sure enough, a folk.

'Well, well, well,' he nodded. 'One of the Valley dwellers.'

'Walking along the bank,' said Skip.

'Exactly. How very interesting.' Potter felt his eyes closing dreamily again.

'Walking in the direction of Heather Hill,' went on Skip cheerfully.

'How nice for him,' muttered Potter gently, slipping into the first of another forty winks.

'Going to the bridge, I shouldn't wonder.'

'I shouldn't wonder at all,' said Potter in his dreams, not wondering at all about anything whatsoever.

'Then I think we should ferry him across,' said

Skip, 'to save him having to walk all the way down the bank, all the way over the bridge, and all the way to wherever he's going once he's crossed it.'

'They certainly are,' said Potter, his toes wriggling comfortably in time with his snore. Skip looked at him.

'What did you say, Potter?'

'You never can tell,' said Potter slowly, and added 'fuff!' because it was difficult to talk and snore at the same time, since breath was required for both.

'Ahoy Valley-folk!' cried Skip at the top of his voice.

Potter sat bolt-upright and caught his left ear on a boat-hook in his surprise. He blinked at Skip.

'Skip Squirrel,' he began patiently, 'I like you. I have always taken a fancy to Squirrels, for they're small and friendly folk. But there are occasions when I could cheerfully—'

'He's heard me!' nodded Skip happily.

'I should imagine the entire Wood has heard you,' grunted Potter, rubbing his left ear. But Skip appeared not to be interested in conversation after all. He was slinging an oar through the port rowlock and pulling on it. Potter turned his head, remembering something having been said about Valley-folk and banks and bridges and all that sort of confusing cross talk.

'Who is it?' he enquired, faintly interested.

'Old Tufty,' said Skip. He plied the oar deeper,

and *Bunty* slewed her slim beams across the current
and nosed obediently into the east bank of the
river.

Old Tufty came over the tow-path and greeted
them. There was a sack over his furry shoulder,
containing something that looked spiky.

'Where are you bound, Tufty?' asked Skip, as
Potter held the boat close with the long hook.

'Old Mr. Nibble said he was doing some thatching

before the Autumn,' said the Valley Squirrel,
'so I've brought him a sack of pine-needles for the
job.'

'Well come aboard,' Potter invited. 'We'll ferry
you over.'

'I'd be glad,' said Tufty—for it was a longish
way down the bank and over the bridge. There was
no other one between the foot of Heather Hill and
the Silver Falls, a good two miles down-stream.

'We caught the Goblins, last night,' said Skip, as
they pulled away from the bank. 'Did you hear?'

'You *caught* them?' gasped Tufty, his ears pricking
up and his tail frisking with astonishment. 'How?'

They told him. And they told him of the feasting
afterwards, and of how the Goblins looked, without
their blue lanterns. He said not a word on their way
to the west bank of the stream, except now and
then—'my my my!' and 'you *don't* tell me!' and
'well-I-*am*-surprised!'

And when they helped him out of the boat, with
his sack of pine-needles for Mr. Nibble's thatching,
he declared he was going to call at Owl's Beech to
see these strangers for himself.

While Skip and Potter went their way down the
Wild River, making for Fallen Elm, the old Valley
Squirrel hurried along the woodland pathways,
calling out a brief 'hello' to any folk as spoke to him
from their doorway, until he reached Woo's Glade.

Woo Owl was at home. So were twenty Goblins,

each with his tall green hat and tunic and buckled shoes. So was Old Stripe and Mole-the-Miller.

'Allow me to introduce you, my dear Tufty,' boomed Woo in his best social tone of boom—'these are the Hobgoblins!"

He flourished an important wing in their direction.

'This, my friends, is Tufty Squirrel, from the Valley.'

Tufty Squirrel blinked in amazement. Though he was a well-mannered old folk, he had difficulty in concealing his scrutiny of these quaint strangers, whom last he had seen as drifting blue lamps through the pine-trees in Sweethallow.

'Please,' he gulped politely, 'to—er—to meet you, I'm sure.'

The leader of the Goblins bowed jerkily, and his green hat wobbled unsteadily on his ears. His fellows bowed with him, while Woo looked on them kindly, and Tuft watched them in surprise. These were certainly different people from those who had annoyed the folk of the Valley, as Potter had said not long ago.

'They were just telling us of their journey from the Erl Kingdom,' explained Old Stripe. So Tuft Squirrel nodded quietly and found himself an empty corner, where he sat down on his sack and listened most attentive. The leader of the Pixies spoke again in his queer, tinkly voice:

' . . . So the Erl King told us that if we wanted to leave his country and to travel, we should have to find another land for our home, as he would never take us back.'

'That's right,' piped another Gnome, nodding so hard that his hat slipped right off the back of his head.

'Well,' went on the leader, whose name was Skimble, 'we still wanted to see the world, and off we went.'

'And we saw it!' nodded another Gnome vigorously, his eyes round with the memory of it. 'And when we tried to go home, we were told to go away again!'

'Just as the Erl King had warned us,' said the leader. He spread his nimble hands and looked at Woo and Stripe and Tuft appealingly. 'We had to have somewhere to live, didn't we?'

'Of course,' said Old Stripe, though he didn't quite understand what all this was leading up to.

'Well, we thought we'd live in Sweethallow Valley, that's all. And the folk wouldn't leave!'

Stripe gave a blink of surprise. Woo Owl frowned deedily among his feathers. Tuft Squirrel raised his brows and said firmly:

'I should think not, indeed!' Then—because these folk were the Woodlanders' guests, after all—he added: 'if you'll pardon my saying so.'

Skimble the Goblin looked amazed.

'But everyone else has always left their home whenever *we've* been around!'

'Huh!' grunted Old Tufty, and added 'if you'll excuse me.'

'M'mm . . . ' murmured Old Stripe, as he began to see what these strange folk meant. Hedgehog the candle-seller had been right—there *was* a reason for the Goblins being abroad. They had been banished from the Erl Kingdom.

'Of course,' he said gently, 'we folk here in the Wood—and the folk of Sweethallow too—think of things in a rather different way.'

'We certainly do!' Tuft couldn't help exclaiming. But he added 'if you'll forgive my saying so.'

'You see,' nodded Woo Owl, trying to break it gently to his guests, 'if *I* were wandering abroad—or if Old Stripe or Tufty were doing the same—*we* would choose a pleasant-looking land to live in, and then we'd knock at the door of any folk who lived there already, and say 'would you mind very kindly if we built a small house in your land, and very kindly lived here?'

'*That's* what we'd say,' nodded the Badger.

'We certainly would!' nodded Old Tufty, 'if you don't mind my very kindly mentioning it.'

The Gnome's voice was plaintive: 'but nobody wants us!'

Old Stripe's was quiet, and gentle, and friendly. 'We do,' he said.

Woo Owl nodded. Even Old Tufty didn't disagree. Skimble the Goblin looked at them in turn; then he looked at his friends, standing about him; then he looked down at his buckled shoes, and held his small hands behind his back.

'Then—then you're very kind,' he whispered.

'And we don't deserve it,' mumbled another Gnome.

'We've done nothing to deserve it,' said a third, shaking his little head and his little green hat at the same time.

A fourth voice piped up suddenly and cheerfully:—

'Then we'll *do* something!'

There was a hush for an instant; then the chorus came:

'We'll do something to deserve your kindness!'

'We'll work—'

'And chop wood and carry water—'

'And sweep and clean and polish and dust—'

'And cook and set the table and—'

'Please!' boomed Woo Owl.

They were quiet again. Woo scratched his ear with a feathery wing-tip and looked in puzzlement at Old Stripe.

'We don't want you to work,' said Old Stripe.

'But we must!' cried the Goblins.

'There's nothing for you to do,' said Old Stripe.

They were abashed. Clearly they would willingly

have turned their tiny hands to any task; but there was none for them.

In the end it was left like this: if there were any work to be done, Old Stripe promised them, then the Goblins would be called upon to help. Until then, they could spend their time how they wished, building themselves a house in the Wood, or gathering stores and such for their own use.

One by one the Gnomes assented to this proposal; but, as one by one they excused themselves from Woo's sitting-room, it was plain that they were off on business of their own. Before Stripe and Woo had been alone with Tufty five minutes, there came the sound of sweeping and polishing from all over the tall, rambling house. Woo's Beech was being given the greatest Spring-clean in all its ancient years—and in high Summertime, too . . .

'You see,' said Woo quietly, as he offered Tufty his big tobacco-jar, 'when these folk have magic powers, they'll turn to all manner of mischief, and no-folk is safe from their tricks. But take away their magic, and they're the nicest little chaps you could wish to meet in a month's journey.'

Old Tufty nodded slowly, a-filling of his pipe with the Owl's fresh-blended baccy. 'They're surely different folk from the blue lamps and lanterns,' he agreed softly. 'I was amazed when I heard what had happened, with the burning of lavender and all.'

The Badger's Dream

'When did you hear?' asked Old Stripe, closing his eyes contentedly in a sunbeam from the windows. Tuft told him how Potter and Skip Squirrel had been kind enough to ferry him over the Wild River from the East bank.

'Ah,' nodded Stripe, and made a soft clicking-noise with his tongue; for many a folk had Potter ferried across in *Bunty* when he happened to be sailing. 'That was kind of him,' he murmured, almost half-asleep.

'I was taking these pine-needles over to Mr. Nibble,' said the Valley Squirrel, 'for his thatching.'

'Ummmm,' nodded the Badger, rocking gently on his heels in the warm sunbeam. Woo Owl glanced at him. From what he knew of his Badgery friend, he was going into a long, deep Think about something-or-other.

'So now I'll be getting along,' said Old Tufty, 'and thank you for your tobacco, Woo Owl, I'm sure.'

'I'm certain,' muttered Old Stripe, talking in his dreams.

'Certain about what?' asked Owl, as Tufty picked up his sack of needles.

'M'mm?' mumbled Stripe. 'I was thinking, that's all.'

'What about?' asked Woo. Because when the Badger had gone off like this before, something quite Brainy and Brilliant was usually found to be forming in his furry old mind.

The Badger's Dream

'About Old Tuft being ferried across the river,' said Stripe, waking up very gently. 'About him, a-doing that.'

Tufty stopped in the doorway, the sack slung over his shoulder.

'Well?' said Owl, persistently.

'Well,' said Stripe, 'I'm thinking of it, that's all. There's something sort of *connected*.'

'Have some baccy,' said Woo, and passed him the jar. If ever the Badger wanted inspiration, he looked for his pipe; so a little bit of baccy might do the trick.

Old Stripe filled his little black pipe, with slow and careful paws, and his forehead was wrinkled as he watched the golden strands being stuffed and pressed comfortably into the small black bowl.

'There's something at the back of my mind,' he nodded, 'about folk being ferried and other folk wanting work to do, and folk being ferried because there's no bridge between Heather Hill and the Silver Falls, and folk wanting work to do because there's twenty of them and that makes forty hands and—'

Woo Owl took a deep and feathery breath, for he felt the Badger needed one. Whatever it was that Stripe was a-thinking of, it was coming more and more clearly to him—though it scarcely sounded like it.

He was silent now, and his paws were not moving

on his pipe. He gazed upwards to the beamed ceiling, and gradually there dawned a slow, furry smile that spread over his stripey old face until it reached the bottom of his chin and the tops of his ears, where it wrinkled with visible glee.

'I know!' he said suddenly.

Woo waited. In the doorway, Old Tufty waited. Until the Badger said softly—

'Come in and close the door, Old Tufty, because this idea is going to interest the Sweethallow folk as much as the Deep Woodlanders.'

So the Squirrel came in, and he closed the door, and he put his sack of pine-needles down again, and he struck a tinder for to light his pipe anew. Then he and Woo Owl drew close to the Badger, and listened to all he'd been thinking about while he was dreaming of it in his warm Summer sunbeam.

Chapter 9

The Bridge across Wild River

THE very next morning, the word went round the wood.

Deep in a copse, a Mole stopped cleaning his windows to talk to a passing Stoat. High in the great green crown of an elm, a Jackdaw stopped sweeping the bough that formed his doorstep, and leaned on his broom while a neighbouring Rook told him the news. Down Silver Birch Hill the Rabbits spoke of it. From Fox End to Heather House, from Badger's Beech to Otter's Island, small tongues went a-wagging while small ears went a-pricking with excitement.

Down in the pine-deep village of Sweethallow, the Chipmunks heard the tidings from the Beavers, for the Beavers had got it from the Gray Squirrels who lived higher on the West Slope near the wood. For Old Stripe's dream was of equal importance to the Valley-Dwellers.

Throughout both lands, upon this Summer's morning, the chattering ran high :

'A bridge, across Wild River?'

'But there's one already, near Heather Hill!'

'It's so far round. A folk must walk a mile along the stream-bank, cross the bridge, and walk another mile back to the middle of the wood.'

'Potter-the-Otter can sometimes ferry folk across.'

'Only sometimes. And when a Valley-Dweller wants to take a barrow to the Wood—or tuther way round—what use is a small boat, even if the Otter chances to be there?'

'Old Stripe is right—we *do* need a bridge! What about the Winter, when the Valley takes peat, and pine-cones, and pine-needles, and fir-cones, for the people in the Wood?'

'And the loads of nuts and berries and herbs that come back, for the Winter stores!'

'It's a wonder the path by the stream isn't worn out, by now!'

'Well it won't be, now—we'll build a bridge!'

'A bridge across Wild River!'

'And the Goblins will help us!'

. . . And so they talked, the Woodlanders and the folk of Sweethallow, of the Badger who'd dreamed of a bridge. Some said it couldn't be built before the Winter came, when the winds and the snows would drive from the North and break the first framework before there was time to strengthen it. Some said that, with the Goblins' help, the river could be crossed before Autumn. There was not one folk, however, who said that it couldn't be built at all, or that there was no need for it.

Old Stripe himself went to see Mr. Nibble of Deep Wood Store; for the old Rabbit was a fine carpenter, and had designed the first bridge to span the River, long ago. It had taken the force of water-spate and flood, of wind and driving hail; it had carried many small feet and the wheels of many loaded barrows, year upon year; and still the timbers were strong and the planking stout and firm.

Old Stripe was here to ask the Rabbit if he would design the second bridge; for it was to be longer (the stream was twice as wide at the place where the pathways of the Valley and the Wood were joined); and it would be wider, the new bridge, so that two barrows might roll side by side.

Old Mr. Nibble, who was carving a tobacco-jar when the Badger called, stopped his work in surprise.

'A new bridge?' he said, fumbling in his fur for to take his pipe and fill it while he talked. 'I've said to Mrs. Nibble, year in and year out—'there ought to be a bridge, between Otter's Island and Stricken Oak.' Many's the time I've said that to her. And every time she'd say—'one day they'll build one, maybe.'

'And now we shall,' nodded Stripe slowly.

Mr. Nibble lit his pipe and sat to watch the smoke for a while as it curled round the bowl and sailed away to the open window.

'Let's go outside,' he said at last, 'and sit in the sunshine. Ye can't go and build a bridge in a small room like this . . . '

So Old Stripe and the carpenter took themselves out to the timber-yard at the back of Deep Wood Store, and sat themselves down on an old gnarled log that was there for just such a purpose. The sun was slanting down through the leaves of the silver-birch, dappling the ancient floor of the timber-yard whose firm clay had been trodden and smoothed by the feet of the Rabbit's ancestors; and by his own. There was the smell of wood in the warm air—of new sawdust and old shavings, of pine-sap and elder-bark, of glue and stain and varnish.

Here was the old Rabbit happiest, for he was at heart a woodman. He knew the trees, and knew what their qualities were. He knew how far would an ash-stem bend before it broke; and how long a beam would weather before it split; and how much weight would a willow-pole bear before it groaned aloud.

He knew how to dress a timber so that water would leave it dry; he knew, indeed, how to build a bridge, and now he took a stick of charcoal and laid a white plank of new-cut birch across his knees. The Badger watched him.

'How wide's the water?' asked the old bridge-builder.

'Ooo—' said Old Stripe, for he didn't know.

'Then we must have the measurement.'

He scratched his head, just between his long brown ears, and said: 'How deep's the stream?'

'Ummm,' murmured the Badger, for he didn't know again.

'Then we must plumb it,' said the Rabbit, nodding slowly in the sunshine. 'And are the banks level?' he said.

Old Stripe got up slowly and tapped out his pipe.

'I think I'd best be going along there,' he said, 'and when I come back I'll tell you all you want to know.'

'Let me go along there with you,' said Mr. Nibble.

Woo Owl, flying above the birches, saw his two friends on their way through the copse, and came down to see where they were off to. And later, as they skirted Badger's Beech, Skip Squirrel joined them, for he'd been a-knocking on Old Stripe's door all morning. And by the time they'd reached the river-bank, several other folk had met with them, and asked to go along to see where they could help. Though no-folk had actually said *'this is the great day'* it *was*, just the same. Today the new bridge would begin taking shape, if only in Mr. Nibble's mind and on his drawing-block.

The Goblins were away beyond Fox End, turning out a disused Rabbit-burrow and decorating it with new ceilings and new doors, new windows and new floors. There did they mean to make their home, and thankful they were for the place.

'Now then,' said Mr. Nibble, as the Woodlanders gathered around him on the river-bank, 'how wide are we?'

'Better fetch a tape-measure,' said someone.

'Better fetch Potter-the-Otter,' said someone else, 'he'll know how wide, for it's his river.'

So Skip Squirrel went along to Fallen Elm to fetch his tape-measure that he used for keeping his bean-patch straight; and Mole-the-Miller went along to fetch Potter.

'All I know,' Potter told him as Mole walked back along the bank, 'is that you have to make eighteen oar-strokes to get from one side to the other. That's if the current isn't fast.'

'I think Mr. Nibble will want to know more accurate than that,' said Mole. But when they reached the group of bridge-planners, Skip Squirrel was back from Fallen Elm with his long tape-measure.

'Now we can make a start!' said the Rabbit, and squinted at the queer markings on the measure. 'Can you read these figures, young Skip?'

Young Skip said he certainly could, and Mr. Nibble said then he was a very clever folk indeed. Skip looked most and exceeding indignant, but he didn't say anything. He might not know much about throwing a bridge across a river, but he'd made

146

the figures on his measure with his own paws; and though nobody else could read them, *he* could.

As the throng of folk waited on the bright green moss of the river-bank, Potter-the-Otter took one end of Skip's tape-measure, and dived into the clear, sunlit ripples, to swim to the other side. Though he swam under-water, which is the swiftest way, his friends could make out his moving shape in the depths of the crystal-clear stream. Below him, his shadow swam over the pebbly bed, where the stones—brick-red, blue, brown and purple—were set in their colourful mosaic.

The surface broke as his head came up, close to the distant bank, showering a spray of silver-falling water-beads into the warm sunshine. And as he climbed to the grass, and tugged the tape-measure clear of the stream, it brought up a frieze of spray that caught a rainbow for an instant before it splashed.

'All ready!' his voice came across the waters.

'What does your end say?' called Skip Squirrel, ready to work out his curious markings.

Potter looked at the words written in blackberry-ink on the woven tape. He looked at them sideways and upside-down, then he peered at them underneath, and finally called:

'It says—UTHER END!'

'Ah,' nodded Skip, conscious of a twinkle in Mr.

Nibble's eye. 'Then our end should be marked THIS END.'

'I don't see that it helps,' suggested Scruff Fox, by way of assisting matters.

'Well it does,' retorted Skip, growing warm under his fur. 'It's no good trying to use a tape-measure if you can't tell which end is which, for a start. Is it?'

'Not a bit,' said someone, thinking this was the right answer to the argument. Skip nodded confidently, looked up at the distant figure of Potter, and called:

'Hold it taut!'

Potter leaned back on the tape, so it should sag less in the middle; while Skip leaned on it from THIS END for the same reason. Old Stripe looked deedily at the marking that was immediately above the edge of the water.

'What does it say?' asked Skip, too intent upon not being pulled into the river by Potter.

'Sixty Wun and a Bit,' read Stripe, frowning.

'How long would the Bit be?' enquired Mr. Nibble.

Skip tried to remember. He knew he'd gone from Sixty Wun to Sixty Four by mistake, when making the figures; and there were two Bits added in between to show this.

'It's sagging so much in the middle,' said Mole-the-Miller, 'that we're bound to make the water wider than it really is.'

The Bridge across Wild River

'Pull harder!' called Woo Owl to Potter, 'it's sagging!'

'*I'm* not wagging it!' complained his distant voice, but he pulled harder, as requested.

'Have a care!' hooted Skip, as he slid towards the river.

Mole grabbed his tufty tail and heaved backwards, while Old Stripe grasped his furry feet and grappled with them, until Skip was airborne and hooting further—

'It's Sixty Wun and a Bit, so we can stop!'

But even before they could stop, the tape broke in the middle and Skip went lurching backwards into Mole, who butted Mr. Nibble in the legs, sending him sprawling on the moss.

Across the river, Potter was seen to be picking himself up from the nettly hollow.

When Mr. Nibble was standing on his feet again, he looked carefully at Skip Squirrel, and said:

'If you folk will excuse me for a little while, I'll just go back to my workshop. I have a tape-measure there.'

And off he went.

*   *   *

Throughout the long Summer day, the folk planned their bridge by the Wild River. In the evening, when Mr. Nibble walked slowly back to his house below Silver Birch Hill, with Old Stripe by his side, he carried under his arm a plank of wood on which were sketched the measurements he needed. The next morning, a meeting was held in Badger's Beech.

So many folk were prepared to help with this gigantic scheme that the Badger decided to use his banqueting-hall for the conference. Chairs were brought from all over the house and taken to the huge high-ceilinged room, where sunbeams slanted warm and golden through the long tunnel-windows that sloped upwards to the moss.

The twenty Hobgoblins came, with their bright buckled shoes new-polished and their hats set straight upon their heads. From Fox End and Heather House, Otter's Island and Owl's Beech, Fallen Elm and Mole Meadow, the Woodlanders came, to sit upon a chair in the Badger's banquet-hall, to perch upon the window-sills, to swing their furry legs from the settle-seats around the hearth. And before the meeting was opened, Old Stripe and his friends Skip and Potter saw that every tankard was brimmed with cool cherry-ale, and that every pipe was filled and lit.

As the fragrant blue smoke rose from the assembled company, each folk stood and raised his pot of ale.

'To the new bridge!' they heard Old Stripe propose, from the end of the banquet-table.

Their tankards clinked, one upon another, with

almost the sound of a peal of muted bells in the Summer-silent room.

'To the new bridge!' they said, and drank deep.

Old Mr. Nibble sat down and shuffled his sheets of parchment on the table, and placed them so that the

Badger could peer at them from one side of him, and Potter-the-Otter from the other.

'Now,' he said; and every voice was quiet. 'We need these for the job: twelve timbers, each fifteen feet high.' He glanced at the Otter beside him.

'They'll have to be sunk in the river-bed, in six pairs. You'll have to see to that, Potter.'

His friend nodded eagerly. He was a true river-folk, and this was his task. No one else in the Wood could dive as deep as he below the ripples, or stay there as long. He would see to the digging of the holes for the timbers, and to their careful placing under-water.

'Two timbers,' went on the carpenter, 'each sixty-five feet long, to span the river. I'll fell those myself, down in a copse of saplings I know, not far from the Birch Hill. Twelve timbers, each ten feet long, as cross-members.' He stabbed the designs with a confident old paw. 'They'll fit above each of the upright pairs, you see?'

Old Stripe peered deedily at the plans. Potter-the-Otter sucked noisily at his pipe, thinking of the cool waters of Wild River, where he would soon be diving to his work. Old Candles, the little Hedgehog, was as interested as any, though tomorrow he would be off again on his pathways through the world, not to return before Autumn.

'Then we need about two hundred planks,' said Mr. Nibble, 'for the floor of the bridge.'

One or two folk gave a gasp, on hearing this. They hadn't realised how much timber must go to the building of a bridge, or how much work was entailed.

'Lastly,' said the Rabbit, 'we shall have six

timbers, each twenty feet long. Each of these will slope against an upright post, on the down side of the bridge, so the current won't press too hard when the stream is in spate.'

Again he pointed to his sketches, and again folk peered over their neighbours' shoulders. Potter-the-Otter gave a slow approving nod.

'We'll need those,' he said, 'for the old river gets rushing strong in the Winter months, when there's snow and such.'

'Then we'll cut our timber stronger than the water,' grunted Mr. Nibble. 'Now has anyone any suggestions to make before we begin?'

Someone said there should be a gate at each end for opening and closing; but someone else said they'd always be left open anyway—and why have them at all?

A Badger said Potter would be bound to have trouble in steering his boat between the posts if he went sailing in the dark; but Potter shook his head and said he'd soon get to know where they stood.

Someone said they should have lamps along the bridge, and suddenly Candles the Hedgehog looked up and said:

'Lamps . . . ' in a very soft voice. For he was a candle-maker.

'I think it's a goodly idea,' nodded Old Stripe.

'Excellent!' boomed Woo Owl. 'A dozen lanterns, strung the length of the bridge?'

'And four bigger ones,' piped up Skimble the Gnome, 'each on a tall post at the end of the bridge!'

'Wonderful!' boomed Woo, expanding in delight. 'Then old Potter won't bump into the beams underneath in the dark—because the lamps will be as bright as stars!'

There was an immediate chorus of approval from the Gnomes and Woodlanders; beneath their voices was the quiet mumble of the folk who had thought of the idea: 'at least I haven't a tape-measure any more, but my brain-box is still with me . . . '

The meeting broke up at twilight, after the great reckoning had been made, of timbers and posts and planks and poles and beams and joists and joints. There were many folk who felt, deep in their minds, that the scheme was far too big to be tackled at all. But then they remembered the old bridge, and how that had seemed just as impossible to throw across the tumbling waters of Wild River.

Old Nibble could do it; and there'd be many a pair of paws to help him, too.

Before Winter, some said. Before Autumn, said others.

'Before *long* . . . ' grunted Mr. Nibble, to whom time meant little. He nodded confidently, bade good-night to Old Stripe at the doorway of Badger's Beech, and took himself off through the trees, his plans rolled firmly underneath his arm.

Slowly he strolled homeward, a small brown

The Bridge across Wild River

Rabbit whose modest name was Nibble. So small was he that a stray leaf, falling from a bough above him, was almost as big as his starlight shadow on the path behind him. But there wasn't a Woodlander who had no faith in him. In his furry old mind, just beneath his two brown furry old ears, there spanned a bridge across a gracious river, stout in its timbers, strong in every beam.

And as he walked homeward to Silver Birch Hill, another small folk was strolling to Owl's Beech, where he would stay the night—his last night in the Wood before Autumn came. Old Candles the Hedgehog was thinking of the bridge, as he smoked of his pipe beside Woo Owl along the pathway. For on the bridge would be lanterns: a dozen lamps and four more, to shine above the river's darkling way.

'And in each lamp,' he breathed softly, half to himself, 'a candle . . . '

'I beg pardon?' asked his friend the Owl.

Hedgehog looked up from the path, scarcely realising he had spoken aloud.

'I said it's a pleasant evening,' he murmured happily, a deep and secret twinkle in his eye.

'Ah,' nodded Owl in agreement. For it was.

Chapter 10

In the Robber Rat's Den

Long before the first timbers were hewn for the building of Sweethallow Bridge, little old Candles the Hedgehog left the land, to seek new pathways through the world, to meet new folk and greet old friends again.

Many from the Woodland went with him up Silver Birch Hill, and as far as Dingle Copse on the Western fringe of the Wood. It was always sad to bid farewell to the candle-seller; but in the Autumn he'd be back, with a fresh store of candles for their lamps.

'And when I see you again,' he told Old Stripe, 'I'll expect to see a fine new bridge across Wild River!'

'We'll do our best for you,' they told him, and shook his small warm paw, one of them by one.

In a few minutes he was a tiny shape down the distance of the pathway; and in a few minutes more he was lost to sight round the foot of the hills.

Times, he thought, had changed in the Wood. The whole world was changing, and new buildings were taking shape while old ones came down. Yet there was one thing about Deep Wood that was different: nothing ever was lost. New folk came to live there, but few folk went away. A new bridge would soon span the river; yet the old one would stay.

He looked up at the clouds that floated across the great blue dome of the skies, and he sniffed the scent of hawthorn as he passed a hedgerow. Summer was everywhere—in the depths of the Woodland, on the great warm faces of the hills and along this very pathway where the earth was smooth and brown, trodden by many small feet of countless travellers.

Hedgehog the candle-seller didn't know, at this moment, where he was bound; and he cared very little. It was enough for him that the air was warm and sunlit, that the path was winding and friendly, and that time meant nothing to him as he wandered the face of the world. Eventually he would arrive at the secret place where always he fetched his candles. It lay many miles from Deep Wood, and many miles from anywhere, for it was a deep cave, snug within the heart of a mountain. Candles the Hedgehog would reach it, some time or other—but *which* time or other he didn't care, no, not a scrap.

All through the balmy day he walked the paths, trundling his barrow of gifts from the Woodlanders. There were new shining pipes, fashioned for him by Old Stripe's skilful paw—cherry-wood and briar, corn cob and clay; and many a box of sweet-blended tobacco—coltsfoot, clover, thyme and honeysuckle. There were fresh made pies, baked in old Mrs. Nibble's favourite oven; toffee-apples from the counter of Deep Wood Store; quaint pots and vases made upon Potter's wheel; and many a choice marrow from Fox End, where Scruff worked at his vegetable-patch the day long.

All through the Summer sun walked Hedgehog, all through the noon. Pies he ate for his lunch-time, and strawberry flan for his tea. By twilight he was a long way from the Wood, and travelling a path strange to his feet. Because of this was he happy— well known and familiar roads were friendly to his feet; but a new way was exciting to him. What lay beyond the next hill, and what beyond the bend?

But now, as twilight deepened beneath a canopy of stars, he sensed a warning in the air. On the horizon there was spread the faint sheen of lights— too many and too bright for any woodland village to spread its lamps.

He was approaching a City, where Men would be, for they had built it from the earth.

For a moment the little folk stopped, and his barrow-wheels ceased their trundling. He had passed through these huge and sometimes terrifying places, where all was noise and excitement and bustle. No Man had ever seen him, for he made sure of that; yet it was always dangerous to walk in places so foreign to him.

For a moment he looked at the twinkle of distant lamps, and he said to his prickly self:

'Hum-hum-hum—I wonder?'

And when he'd finished his wondering, he still couldn't make up his prickly old mind whether to make a detour round the City on the horizon, or to pass through it in the cover of the coming night. So he started off again, to reach the last hill-brow before the City's outskirts.

The starglow was brighter from the sky, when he topped the gentle rise. And the lights in the nearer distance were like the stars' reflection on the dim green velvet of the earth.

For another moment he looked down at the clustered buildings, and watched the sheen of light that hung above them. Faintly to his ears there came the murmur of the streets—and something tingly went sparking through his limbs and there was a catch of excitement in his breath as he made up his mind and trundled off with his barrow down the last long slope to the Town.

What he would do there he did not know. What he would find he could only guess. He knew only that the Mountain he must finally reach for his new supply of candles lay southward, and so did this City. He must pass through the streets, some-how, and somehow must cross the great river that he had glimpsed on the far side of the buildings.

It was night when he reached the first few cottages that bordered the wider roadway. From now he must be cautious, for no Man must glimpse the small prickly form who rolled his tiny barrow through the starlight.

Men moved along the road in their great noisy carriages; but no Hedgehog was to be seen. As the huge lamps came rumbling nearer, he skipped into the deep shadow of a hedge, dragging his cart behind him. When a loud, gruff voice reached his alert little ears, he melted to the shelter of a building.

He was strolling cheerfully down a long alley-way between buildings as tall as the moon, when a voice came from the darkness of a grating in the path—

'Hhssttt! Go careful there!'

It was a Town Mouse, warning him of the Men.

'I will, I will,' called the candle-seller softly, and wheeled his barrow more slowly to stop its tiny rumbling. Lanterns were above him now, as tall as trees and as bright as a Summer sun. And when he reached the end of the alley he came upon cobble-stones, and had great difficulty in wheeling his barrow over their irregular humps.

He paused, motionless, as a sudden gray shape loomed from a darkened doorway, and two glittering eyes of emerald-green winked within a yard of him.

In the Robber Rat's Den

'Go stealthy, there . . . ' said the big grey Cat, 'you'll find Men about if you're not cautious.'

He came up to Hedgehog and lent a paw with the barrow, hauling it over the rest of the cobbles until they were standing upon a smoother pathway.

'Thank you, I'm sure,' said Hedgehog, as the Cat walked away with his tail poised and his great eyes blinking in the lights.

'Queer folk, are the Cats,' thought Candles, as he trundled his cart down the way. 'They live among the Men as though they like them. Too fond of comfort, I suppose—though that fellow was kind and friendly.'

He made his way through the streets, sometimes alone, sometimes with a Town-Mouse or a Black Rat accompanying him. The City-Folk always recognised a country visitor, and usually gave him safe conduct for a while through the buildings of the Men.

'How far is the river?' he asked, as a Black Rat prepared to take his leave of him.

'Oh, about a mile more,' he said, stroking his smart black whiskers. 'Straight down the road here, to the left, and you'll find the Docks.'

'The Docks,' nodded Hedgehog, for he knew of such places. 'Thank you, Black Rat, I'm sure.'

He went onwards, alone again, passing beneath the great shining lamps, ducking to a doorway when a Man went by, or squeezing his barrow into a crevice and crawling beneath it to hide himself for a moment. His little heart went a-thumping more than once as a huge pair of tramping boots came swinging near, or a great carriage thundered by along the roadway.

This land was foreign to Old Candles. He feared it, and he was excited by it. The noise was sometimes frightening, yet always of immense interest to him. And he had been a traveller since a time when he just couldn't even remember, and knew most of the ways of the Men.

He could already smell the strange scent of the Docks. It was a mixture of oil and steam, and wet rope. Already he could glimpse the tall mast of a ship as it reared even higher than the rooftops of the Town.

When the roadway gave on to cobblestones again, he drew his barrow to a smooth little track at the side, and went down the hill, seeing now the glint of still water between the buildings. In a matter of minutes he would be by the water's edge, and would find out the width of it, and how to cross with his barrow.

But minutes were made of many seconds: and each second was a danger to little Hedgehog on this foreign soil.

He was moving between two vast gate-posts, not fifty yards from a group of wharves, when a shadow seemed to come from nowhere, and a voice hissed:

In the Robber Rat's Den

'Halt! Who are you, there?'

Hedgehog's heart went pitter-pitter-bump; but he kept his head and his courage. It was no Man's voice, anyhow, for it was not of their strange language.

'I am Hedgehog,' he said simply, peering into the gloom to see what manner of folk this shadow could be.

'Ha!' said the folk, and came forward. He squinted at the traveller with black and beady eyes. His fur was brown and glossy, and about his throat was tied carelessly a red-and-white spotted kerchief. Around his waist was a wide leather belt, and carried there was a wicked-looking holster, the shape of a knife. Boots glimmered dully in the gloom —boots that reached to the Robber Rat's knees, and clumped as he stamped his foot.

'What Hedgehog?' he asked softly, 'from the country?'

'From nowhere,' said the prickle-folk stoutly, 'that is your business.'

The Robber Rat stamped his foot twice more, and in an instant two more shadows sprang from the gloom, and ranged themselves by his side.

'Come with us,' they told Candles, 'and bring your barrow, too . . . '

Now Hedgehog was a brave enough folk, for all his age and his size. Many a time he had tackled bigger creatures than these, and lived to laugh at

them. But he was as wise as his countless years. The
robbers numbered three already; and the traveller
was but one. At any moment they might summon
help from their rascally friends, and then he would
be lost.

'Very well,' he said evenly. 'I'll go with you.'

There'd be a chance, later, to outwit these folk, he knew, if he gave himself time to work a plan for their undoing.

Two of them moved to his barrow, and each took a handle. The third gripped Hedgehog's arm, and led him into the shadows. He expected a long journey to begin, and was more than prepared to get rid of these unwelcome companions on the way; but within a minute or two he found himself walking down a sharp wooden slope, and heard the clang of a gate behind him.

Already he was in the den of the robber-folk, and it was too late to struggle.

Three loud knocks sounded immediately in front of him, where the two Rats stood with his barrow. He could see not a thing in the darkness here, but guessed they had come to a door.

A gash of yellow light split the gloom of a sudden, and hinges shrieked in the silence.

'Who are you?' growled a voice, as a great Rat stood silhouetted against the light.

'Friends,' squeaked Hedgehog's captors, 'bringing a traveller to our Chief!'

The door was thrown open wider, and Hedgehog's cart was wheeled through into the light.

'Ha!' cried a voice, 'bringing a load of gifts for me, too!'

Candles followed—or rather was pushed from

behind; and the door was slammed fast. He stood for a moment, his eyes blinking in the strong light, until he could make out where he was.

The room was high, and narrow, and the walls were old and crumbling. Crates, boxes and odd spars of timber lay strewn around; and here and there was a candle, burning in the neck of a black, dirty bottle. There were five Rats in all, and each wore some sign of his rascally calling—a scarf or a belt or a pair of sea-boots. Each carried a weapon, too—a knife, a stick, or a short truncheon.

'Sit down!' ordered the Chief Rat, who wore a scarf *and* belt *and* boots, *and* a black patch over one beady-bright eye.

Hedgehog looked round, and another Rat drew up a crate for him. He sat upon it, and was grateful, for he hadn't stopped walking since twilight, before he had come to the City.

'Now then!' he heard the Chief Rat, 'where are you from, Hedgehog?'

'From here and there,' said he, 'and everywhere.'

There was a heavy silence. The four Rats drew close about him, while the Chief sat lounging upon a sugar-box in the middle of the room, glaring with his one bright eye.

'And what were you doing there?' he asked ferociously. Hedgehog chuckled, deep inside his prickles. These folk were all thunder-and-bluster, with their absurd questions.

166

'Oh,' he replied simply, 'this and that, and the other.'

The Chief Rat pondered over this, and twirled his fine shiny whiskers.

'And who is this barrow for?' he asked, his voice as gruff as he could manage. 'With all these gifts?'

'Not for you,' retorted Hedgehog swiftly.

The Chief Rat got up from his sugar-box and inspected the load with a suspicious paw.

'Food,' he said, and his bright eye gleamed. 'And new pipes—and tobacco!' He fixed Hedgehog with a glare, and growled—'where are you taking these, hey?'

'Away with me,' said Candles, 'when I go.'

'You are, are you?' bellowed the Chief Rat. His four confederates leapt up and said:

'Sshhh! You'll have the Men here, with that noise!'

'Sit down,' said their leader; but he said it very softly. He sat down himself, and looked at Hedgehog again.

'So you're a traveller,' he nodded slowly, trying to think of what to say next. 'And where are you going?'

'Over the river,' said Hedgehog.

'Impossible! It's too wide.'

'There's no river too wide for me to cross,' said Old Candles simply.

The Robber Rats glanced at one another. After a long silence, the Chief said:

'Now see here, Traveller. We've been trying to cross that river for months, because it's too dangerous, living so close to these pesky Men in their pesky City. So if *we* can't ford the water, I don't see how *you* can!'

Old Candles thought quickly, as he met the Chief Rat's gaze, eye for eye. He didn't for the life of him know how to cross the river, for it would be many times wider than the stream that ran through the trees of Deep Wood. But if these Robber Rats were on his side, and helped him with his barrow, there might be a way . . .

'I'll make a bargain with you,' he said boldly. 'And you'll realise I'm going out of my way to help you. I can cross the river easily enough without this cart of mine; but it's a little bit cumbersome, you understand.'

'We understand,' their leader nodded eagerly.

'Then,' said Hedgehog, 'I'll get you over the water, if you'll help me with the barrow.'

Without glancing at his brothers, the Chief Rat smote his paw.

'Done!' he cried, and his voice echoed in the rafters.

'Hssttt!' said the other four, 'you'll have the Men here!'

'Drat them pesky Men!' he retorted, 'we'll be away beyond the river by morning light! And Hedgehog will show us how!'

In the Robber Rat's Den

Hedgehog said nothing. He had given his word, and he would find a way, somehow. He must cross the river himself, and it mattered not to him whether he took five Rats with him or fifty. They'd be a great help to him; it was one matter to jump a ferry and hide until it landed at the far bank, but quite a different matter to get a barrow on board, and a loaded one, at that.

'Good old Hedgehog!' said the one who had first waylaid him.

'Excellent fellow!' nodded a brother.

The Chief Rat rose from his sugar-box, and ordered them to strike their camp. Then he looked at Old Candles.

'When do we leave, Cap'n Hedgehog?'

Captain Hedgehog thought quickly.

'At midnight!' he said. 'First I'll have to go and make the necessary arrangements—' and he nodded knowingly for their benefit—'then I'll be back to join you at twelve o'clock.' He looked at his barrow, and added: 'I'll leave my belongings here—and mind you keep them safe.'

'We shall,' they assured him. He nodded solemnly.

'If there's one thing missing when I get back,' he warned them, 'you'll never know the secret of crossing that river from me—you understand?'

They did; or they said they did.

'Good. Then show me the way out of this den of yours.'

In the Robber Rat's Den

Meekly the Chieftain made for the door, and held it wide for him. His voice was a gruff whisper:

'Straight up the wooden slope, my friend, and open the grille at the top.' He frowned slightly as an afterthought struck him—'what arrangements are these you've got to make, might I ask?'

'You might,' said Hedgehog casually, 'and I'll tell you, for it's simple enough. I'm going out to order a ship.' He snorted as scornfully as he knew how. 'Unless of course you mean to swim across?'

He heard the gasps of the Robbers as he strolled through the doorway, and chuckled softly inside his prickles as he climbed the slope to the iron gate. But, once in the narrow street beyond, where the lamplight shed gleaming down, the chuckle died.

It was all very fine and dandy, going out into the night to order a ship—but how exactly was it done?

His small shadowy figure slipped without a sound down the cobbled hill, to where the stars were glittering upon the black, silent waters of the river.

There must be a way. And if anyfolk could find it, then *he* could, or his name wasn't Hedgehog.

And it was.

Chapter 11

Dwarf Mountain

BEFORE the chimes of midnight sounded from the Town Clock, Hedgehog was back at the Robbers' den, just as he had promised.

They greeted him eagerly.

'Have you ordered a ship for us?' asked the Chief Rat, half expecting the traveller to say no—for he was a small folk, and the ships of the Men were mighty.

'I have,' said Candles casually. 'A fine ship, sound in her beams and tall in her mast. Are you ready?'

They tried to conceal their admiration; but failed.

'I must admit you know your way around the world,' said the Chief Rat. 'I must admit *that.*'

Candles shrugged his prickly shoulders.

'Oh,' he said, 'a folk has to know what he's doing, you know.'

He looked at his barrow, and made sure there was not one thing taken from it.

'We'll need a tarpaulin,' he told them, 'to keep the load inside when we swing it up to the decks.'

Dwarf Mountain

They were even more amazed, but made haste to find a stout cover of canvas, and to rope it round securely. If the Hedgehog said he had a ship waiting, then they were ready to believe it, and to join him on board. But what the secret of his boldness was, they didn't attempt to wonder.

The secret of it was that Old Candles had been lucky. The first folk he had looked for when he had left the Robbers' den was a sailor—and he'd found one, leaning on the dockside a-smoking of his pipe in the starlight.

'A ship?' he'd said, and he'd thought over the matter for a while. 'Well,' he'd told the traveller, 'there's a ship moving out at one in the morning, for the river-mouth.'

'Will it be stopping at the far bank?' Candles had asked him.

'Ay—takin' on stores at the Barn Wharf.'

Hedgehog had thanked him, and had offered a fill of baccy for his pipe before they'd parted.

The worst of the problem was over. How the barrow, five Rats and himself were going to board the ship, he didn't know at all. But they would, somehow, for he must cross the river, and they must help him with his burden.

'She leaves in an hour,' he told the Rats, 'and the Captain will put us ashore at the Barn Wharf.'

'You spoke to the *Captain*?' gasped their leader, blowing a ditty on his whiskers in surprise.

Hedgehog nodded easily. For all he knew, the Sailor Rat he'd spoken to might well have been the captain of a small boat of his own.

The Robbers wasted no more time. Long before one stroke chimed from the great clock in the Town, the six of them were standing on the quay-side, beneath the mighty shape of the boat that was to take them over the wide waterway—or so Old Candles hoped.

They looked to him for orders. Though he was half the size of the Chief Rat, and wore no kerchief or belt or knee-boots, the situation was clearly his to command, so great was their respect for his powers.

Now he was really nonplussed. He had found the ship, from the Sailor Rat's careful directions; and they were in time, with several minutes in hand. But there remained the little question of boarding it . . .

'Now we shall have to go quietly,' he said in a whisper. 'The Captain knows we're coming aboard, of course, but if we travel as ordinary passengers we'll have to pay the price. So we'll stow ourselves below decks, and nothing will be said—you understand?'

They did—and respected his cleverness. They would cheerfully have paid a fee for the crossing, by whatever goods they had to offer; but to travel for no price at all was a far better thing.

'Where do we board her, then?' whispered the Chieftain gruffly, respecting the need for stealth.

Hedgehog glanced around them in the starlight, and saw a long mooring-rope, stretching and sagging from the ship's stern to a stanchion on the quay.

'Up there,' he said simply, hoping it was going to be as simple as he'd made it sound.

One of the Rats shook his head quickly.

'No good, Hedgehog,' he said. 'They've slung discs on the rope—look—you can see them from here. How do we climb round those, I'd like to ask?'

Hedgehog sensed that they were beginning to suspect that this little adventure had not been planned quite so openly as he was leading them to believe.

'And how do we get your barrow of goods up the rope—*and* round the discs,' said their leader, 'even if we could do it ourselves?'

Old Candles felt decidedly cheerless about this new problem; but he had managed things well so far, and he did not intend giving up at the last moment.

'If you keep pestering me with your stupid questions,' he said sternly, to give himself time to think, 'I'll lead the way. Or do you want to stay on this bank of the river?'

'We don't!'

'We certainly don't!'

'We'll give you anything—everything we have—if you'll take us across!'

'Fiddlesticks!' he snorted, 'you'd throw me into the water as soon as look at me if you thought it would do you any good.'

'No, we give our word—'

'We promise you—'

'*Quiet!*' said Hedgehog with as much of a frown as he could muster on his prickly brow. 'Less of this noise!'

They fell silent at once, and hung their lean brown heads. Hedgehog sized up the situation swiftly, worked out a plan that was better than no plan at all, and said:

'Now listen carefully. We'll climb the rope as far as the first disc, and taken for granted we can do *that*, we'll tie a length of cord to the rope this side, and one of us can climb down it as far as the bottom of the disc. Then he just slings the free end of the cord over the rope the *other* side, brings the end down, and ties it. What could be easier than that?'

One of them was just about to say several things might be much easier than that; but he caught a look in the Hedgehog's eye, and thought better of speaking. They worked it all out for themselves, and finally the Chief said:

'That's the cleverest dodge I've heard for a long time, traveller!'

'Then don't waste precious minutes talking about it,' said he briskly. 'Up we go now! Bring the cord from round that canvas on the barrow!'

But, even as they climbed and the Chief Robber did as he was instructed to bridge the disc, Hedgehog was trying to think up a way of hauling his barrow on board.

Not long before one o'clock, four Rats and Candles himself stood on the deck of the mighty ship, where many a lamp was burning bright, and many a sea-boot was tramping loudly on the planking.

'Now make haste!' breathed Hedgehog. 'Fetch a rope from one of the lockers and bring it here!'

One of them scampered off to the nearest hatchway; for a Rat knows as much about the inside of a ship as any Man. When he returned, breathless but with a long coil of cord about his shoulders, Hedgehog ordered:

'Sling it down to your friend below!'

As the rope was whirled and sent snaking down in the starlight, a Man's voice bellowed from the bridge of the ship.

'Make haste!' snapped Hedgehog, 'they're getting ready to sail!'

From below them they heard a faint squeak as the fifth Rat caught the rope and held the end firmly in his paws.

'He knows what to do,' murmured Old Candles, 'but he'll have to be fast about it.'

The Rat on the quayside knew the urgency, for he also had heard the sounds of activity on board. The very last thing he wished to happen was for himself to be left stranded when the ship sailed.

Lashing the end of the rope to the barrow-handle, he tied a second length, and held it coiled in his paws.

'Haul up!' he squeaked, waving to his friends above.

There came, like a gigantic echo from the bridge, the voice of a Man shouting orders for casting-off the mooring-ropes.

'Quick, quick, quick!' urged Hedgehog, 'we're nearly too late!'

'Let's leave the barrow,' growled the Chief Rat, 'and get our friend aboard while there's time!'

'Without the barrow,' snapped Candles, 'not a single one of us sails! Now haul up there!'

By his tone, they knew he meant business. Their efforts were redoubled on the rope. As they heaved the barrow from the dockside, their friend below them paid out the second rope, so it shouldn't swing and crash against the beam of the ship. At last it swung clear, turning slowly on the end of the rope.

'Let go!' called Hedgehog, risking the Men hearing his small voice. 'Come aboard!'

The Robber on the quay needed no second order. He was springing for the great mooring-rope as his four friends went on hauling up the barrow to the deck, Hedgehog working swiftly with the rest of them.

There came now the heavy tramp of sea-boots

along the planking, and the huge shape of a Man loomed up in the lamp-light.

'One more heave!' panted Old Candles desperately. He knew that without any warning the Robbers might leave the rope and drop the barrow if they thought the danger was too close. But the traveller had told them: they wouldn't sail unless the cart went with them. And they had a great respect for the traveller.

As the little barrow bumped against the rails, the fifth Robber came aboard, dropping to the deck from the mooring-rope and lending a paw with the work even as the sailor bent over the stanchion, not a dozen yards away. On the dockside, another Man was loosening the rope, ready for hauling-in.

Hedgehog gave no further command. The Rats had sense of their own to see what must be done next. They had to reach shelter, without wasting a second. Yet, even though they realised this, they grabbed the handles of the cart and helped Old Candles wheel it across the smooth deck to the shadow of a hatchway. The rumble of it was loud; but not so loud as the shouting of the Men as they prepared to move off with their ship.

Orders were being bellowed from the bridge. Ropes were skimming and smacking down onto the decks as they were cast off. A siren hooted with startling suddenness; and the gang-plank rattled inboard on its rollers.

Dwarf Mountain

Deep in the engine-room there throbbed the machinery, so that every plank trembled to its steady murmur. Only the skies were silent and aloof, as the myriad stars swam in their dark spaces, a million miles away and more.

As the great clock of the Town came chiming across the night, echoing among the sleeping roof-tops and fading over the river, six small folk were crouched safely under the shelter of a locker in the stern; and the Chief of the Robber Rats shook the traveller warmly by the paw.

'I never believed you could do it, Hedgehog!' he said gruffly.

The prickle-folk said nothing, except, deep down in his secret thoughts: 'Neither did I . . . '

But he had.

*   *   *

Many a day and night had passed since his meeting with the Robber Rats, when Old Candles saw at last the Mountain that reared to the south above the sunlit fields. Many an adventure he had had, before his eyes had scanned the horizon and seen his goal.

The sun was warm on his back as he trundled his barrow down the sloping path; and was warm still on his shadow that was thrown by the reflection of the Mountain Pool as he skirted the calm blue water.

By evening he reached the winding pathway that

led to the cave where lived the two candle-makers, the Dwarves who were his oldest friends. As he climbed the steep path dragging his cart behind him, for that way was easier, he could see the blue spiral

of smoke that rose from a chimney, hidden in the folds of the mountainside.

He looked down, at last, upon the sleeping fields far below him, where the pathway ran as a faint brown cord drawn loosely across the land. His feet were on the smooth earthen porch, and his small paw was raised to the great bell-rope that hung beside the ancient door. And as the rope jerked, dancing in the twilight, he heard the distant chiming of the bell, deep within the mountain's heart.

It seemed a long time to him, as he waited for his friends; but he knew the mountain well, and knew of its rambling passages that led down to the secret cave where lived the Dwarves.

There sounded of a sudden the quick patter of feet, and two excited voices as the bolts were drawn back on the other side.

Old One and Tuther seldom had visitors to their dwelling; and maybe they had guessed the meaning of the tolling bell. Hedgehog had not been to see them since before summer, and now autumn would soon be about the land.

They greeted him with smiles of welcome wreathing their wrinkled faces; they bustled him inside, and his barrow with him. And before he had time to tell them how he had fared since last they saw him, he was entering the Cave where they lived and worked, and passed their years together.

'Sit down, sit down!' cried Old One, and drew up a great chair whose arms almost rose above Hedgehog's prickly head when he settled into it.

'Where have you been?' asked Tuther, and plied him with tobacco for his pipe. 'What have you seen, and what lands have you been through?'

Little Old Candles sat him in comfort in the great

G

chair, wriggling his tired feet that did not even touch the floor as he sat talking with his friends.

They were scarcely taller than he, for they were Dwarves; but the cavern was huge, and was every bit as cosily-furnished as Old Stripe's banquet-hall in Badger's Beech. There were shelves, ranging the walls, and many an ancient book leaned against a fellow beneath the candle-brackets. In the centre of the cave was a large round hearth, and the smoke from the sweet-smouldering logs went upwards to the mouth of the great chimney immediately above.

Shafts were tunnelled through the earth to the face of the mountainside, so that by daytime the room was filled with sunshine, and with starlight now, as the three friends talked over a pipe and a spot of honey-brew. Racks there stood below one wall, heavy with tools and beakers and pots of candle-wax; and row upon row of moulds there were, so that a candle could be made to any shape— long and straight or fat and twisted, wrinkled ones or smooth.

It was here that the candles were fashioned for the dwellings in Deep Wood. In Badger's Beech and Fallen Elm there would burn lamps, in the coming Autumn, whose light was made by the skilful movement of a dwarfy hand, here in the mountain cave. And Hedgehog the Traveller, with his small barrow, would see that it was so.

Dwarf Mountain

'Tell us of Deep Wood,' said Old One, and Tuther said:

'Tell us about Old Stripe—'

'And his friend Potter-the-Otter!'

'And Woo the Owl, of Owl's Beech!'

So Hedgehog told them of the woodland folk, and of their doings among the distant trees. And when he had finished, he looked with a twinkle deep in his kindly eyes, and said:

'There's some rather special news to come, and your help will be wanted.'

'Our help? How can we help?'

Old Candles told them of the fine new bridge that was to span the Wild River, and of the lanterns that would shine above the water there.

'Big lanterns,' he said, 'the biggest in all the Wood. And they'll need the biggest candles you have ever dreamed upon.'

'Candles for a bridge!' they gasped, and waited to hear more.

As the starlight shone pale through the long slanting windows, they lit the lamps around the walls, until the cavern was warm with light; and when the embers of the hearth were roused from their slumber with fresh logs, there danced shadows round the room as the flames leapt and gathered beneath the great chimney.

Far into the night they talked, and planned how to make the biggest candles they had ever dreamed upon. Old One was a-smoking of a new-made pipe, brought by Hedgehog from Badger's Beech; and Tuther was trying a new brand of baccy, devised by the Badger's skill.

This mountain, and this land, was far from the trees of Deep Wood; yet the folk who lived there were talked of now, between these three small friends. And while the candle-makers smoked a pipe, fashioned in the workshop in Old Stripe's house, they had many a smooth crimson candle ready to light that very room when Autumn came to the trees.

Though the Dwarves had never seen the Wood, they knew almost every tree and every woodlander, through the quiet words of the traveller who was with them now.

Hedgehog had never told the Badger and his neighbours the secret of his travels to the Mountain; they could only guess where their candles came from. But one day, maybe, he would tell them of the Dwarves, and of the secret of the mountain cavern.

One day, maybe, he would tell them; but there was no hurry.

Chapter 12

The Runaway Timber

THERE were sounds of busyness in Deep Wood. The rise and fall of a hammer was heard from Silver Birch Hill, where Old Nibble was driving a peg. In Shingle Spinney, nearby the River and Marten's Elm, there sounded the hewing of wood, for many folk were there, felling saplings for the new bridge.

In Deep Wood Store, old Mrs. Nibble was making sandwiches and honey-ale; and two small Rabbits were trotting to and fro through the woodland, carrying good things for the folk who laboured, and something winking in a cool brown tankard for their thirst.

Potter-the-Otter was nowhere to be seen; for he was below the surface of the Wild River, digging into the bed of pebbles to drive deep holes for receiving the first upright posts. There helped him many Water-Voles, and even Mole-the-Miller was with him, for he was a fine little swimmer when he chose.

The Runaway Timber

All over the Wood there came these sounds of toil; but chiefly from Shingle Spinney, for it was here that most of the timber was being taken.

Skip Squirrel, Scruff Fox, and Old Stripe were there, together with Skimble the Gnome and some of his sprightly fellows. Old Nibble was on his way there even now, for he had stopped his peg-driving behind the shop.

The timber had been chosen by the old carpenter, the day before; he knew the worth of a tree when he saw one, and he chose them well. Already Skip and Skimble were working with a great woodman's axe: Skip would swing it mightily, and as the handle swept sideways, small Skimble would go a-pushing it until the blade met the trunk of the tree. Scruff Fox did very little but watch out for their safety, with an occasional: 'Watch your head, Skimble' or 'Mind your tail, Skip Squirrel!'

Old Stripe stood by, anxiously regarding the great blade as it swung lustily towards the tree, struck with a deep splitting of timber, and was drawn clear with a wince of sap-moist splinters. It was lunch-time when Skip stood back and looked at his tree. Other folk were still hewing around him, where the saplings reared tall and willow-straight; but Skip was nearly through.

'What d'you think, Mr. Nibble?' he asked, eyeing the great V-shaped grooves round the bottom of the bole.

The Runaway Timber

Old Nibble cocked his head on one side, and looked at things. Then he cocked it on the other, and looked at things from there. And when he'd decided that they were much of the same thing, he said:

'Well.'

'Shall we hew some more?'

'No,' he said. 'For one thing it's about lunch-time, so we'll have to see what Mrs. Nibble has brought us. And for another thing we'd best leave that timber for hauling down, else the breeze'll fetch her on top of our heads.'

So the folk stopped work for their lunch, and sat to have it upon a mossy bank, not far from where the ripples winked and glimmered in the sunshine on their way down the river to the Falls. Mrs. Nibble had prepared a light snack for each of them—just a couple of mushroom pies, a dozen oatcake patties and gooseberry flan to finish.

Old Mr. Nibble ate his pies, and his patties, and his flan; then he poured a golden cascade of honey-ale into his drinking-pot, and sat to sup in the sun. After which, he refilled his tankard and supped again; then he stuffed with baccy his corn-cob pipe, lit it with a tinder-flame, and closed his eyes in the warmth of the early afternoon. Within a moment the smoke had stopped drifting from the bowl; and in a moment more the pipe fell gently and quietly from his mouth and skidded down his chest, until it arrived safely between his feet, which were wriggling in their dreams.

Old Stripe, leaning heavily on Scruff Fox, was fast asleep himself; and so was Scruff. Skimble the Gnome had taken his fellows to the place where Potter was digging the holes in the stream-bed.

Skip Squirrel was dozing, certainly, but one of his tufty grey ears was quivering very slightly at the top of its tip, for all the world as though he were about to listen to something, if only he could remember what it was. And one of his soft grey eyelids was not *quite* closed, as though he were ready to peer at anything if only a folk would show it to him.

He was thinking, maybe, too hard about the bridge that was being built from the trees of Shingle Spinney, to slip into dreams so easily as had his friends. In fact he dozed no more than an hour, when his eagerness to carry on grew so great as to get the better of him.

'Hey-ho-hummm,' he murmured, opening his eyes. He blinked up at the sunshine, and was glad to see it still there.

'Tum-ttidle-ttiddle-um-tummm,' he added, and looked around him. 'Just as I *thought*,' he said. For there was Old Stripe, with his whiskers shining in the sunbeams as they trembled to his snores. And there was Scruff Fox helping him. Even Mr. Nibble seemed to have forgotten that they were in the middle of Great Things.

The Runaway Timber

'Huh!' said Skip Squirrel severely.

But no-folk said anything, such as 'What?' or 'did you say anything?' or 'What *sort* of Huh d'you mean?'

'All fast asleep!' said Skip indignantly, and got to his small furry feet.

He looked down at Old Stripe, very very seriously. Old Stripe looked at nothing whatsoever for his eyes were tightly closed; and he didn't look a *bit* serious about anything.

'Old Stripe!' said Skip loudly, and waited.

After a long time, the Badger began rocking his head gently against Scruff Fox's shoulder; and faintly he murmured:

'Ah . . . '

'Wake up!' said Skip. 'Scruff Fox!'

'What for?' asked Old Stripe dreamily, without opening his eyes. 'Why don't you let him sleep?'

'You too,' said Skip firmly.

'Me too,' nodded Old Stripe in his Badgery dreams, 'why don't you let me too sleep too, I believe.'

Old Stripe was given to talking like this when he was fast asleep. Skip Squirrel knew it. He looked at Stripe and looked at Scruff, and looked at Mr. Nibble. Then he cupped his paws and shouted:

'Stand clear below! Tree falling!'

The effect was immediate. Old Stripe gave a careful sniff in the middle of his snore; and Scruff raised a weary paw and scratched the tip of his nose.

Skip Squirrel looked at Mr. Nibble, who was sleeping soundly. Then he stumped off in the direction of more folk, in case there were any awake enough to help him bring his tree down.

It was mid-afternoon when there were sufficient willing paws to help Skip Squirrel. Four ropes were rigged to the doomed sapling; one from each of the four trees nearest to it. Then the bole was cut clean through, and the tree lowered slowly to the ground by the ropes.

'First one down!' cried Skip, and untied the ropes with busy paws. 'Now for moving it to the place where they're building!' He looked at Mr. Nibble. 'How?' he asked simply.

'Best thing,' said the old Rabbit, eyeing the mighty timber on the ground, 'would be to fetch two barrows, and put one under the front and t'other under the back, and push it along the path.'

'That would be fine,' nodded Old Stripe, 'if we had two barrows.'

'As we haven't,' said Scruff, 'it's not so easy.'

Old Nibble put his head on one side.

'Ah,' he said wisely, 'I'd forgotten that.'

'In any case,' said Woo Owl, who had flown down to help them after lunch, 'we'd never get that length of timber round some of the bends. They're too sharp.'

The Runaway Timber

'Then we'll use the river,' said Old Stripe, filling his cherry-wood in the sunshine.

'The river?' said Skip. The Badger nodded.

'Drag it to the water—it's only a few dozen yards. Then it will float down-stream to where Potter wants it.'

'Excellent!' said Mr. Nibble.

'Amazing!' boomed Woo Owl.

'As long as we steer it past Otter's Island,' Skip nodded. 'Shall we make a start?'

'Need some ropes,' said a Rabbit, and began tying the hauling-cords onto the timber again. It was fully twenty feet long, and weighed heavily. But the river was not far from the Spinney, and before tea-time the great log was ready for rolling into the ripples.

'Are we all set?' asked Skip, who regarded this mighty piece of wood as his especial charge.

Old Nibble nodded.

'As soon as she floats,' he said, 'someone will have to go down-stream to warn Potter and his friends.'

'I'll go,' said a Stoat, and turned away into the trees at once. The others, holding the huge log back from the bank with ropes, took the final signal from old Mr. Nibble, let go their ropes, and watched, a second later, the timber go rolling down the bank and into the water, sending up a mighty shelf of spray while the log sank, and then reappeared, floating swiftly.

'A handsome piece of wood,' commented Mr. Nibble, nodding his head and his long brown ears as well. The new bridge was well begun.

'Woo Owl,' said Old Stripe, his gaze following the log as it was carried rapidly down-stream with the strong current, 'I should fly along and warn Potter, if I were you—just look at that log!'

'It's travelling fast!' said Skip; and a note of alarm sounded in his furry voice. 'Better catch up!'

'Better catch up!' squeaked a Weasel, and was off down the bank, racing the log that rolled majestically along in the swirling ripples.

'No time to be lost!' said Woo Owl, and spread his wide wings. In an instant he was beating swiftly over the tree-tops, and already beginning a long, fast glide downwards to the spot where Potter worked in the river.

'It's going to hit Otter's Island!' cried someone, as they raced along the bank.

'The current will carry it past!' said another, his breath coming fast as he ran. Old Stripe trotted by the side of Mr. Nibble; and both their pipes were out. Skip Squirrel ran alongside Scruff Fox, and they said not a word between them. The log would be all right; the current was not *that* swift. Potter would be warned in time by Woo Owl, and there'd be plenty of folk to stop the timber as it slipped along between the banks. But, just the same, Skip and Scruff were wondering if it wouldn't be wiser to

make more careful preparations, when next they
went floating great tree-trunks down-river.

Woo Owl was the only folk who saw the log
reach Otter's Island, for his friends had not caught
up with it yet, and Potter's party didn't even know
it was coming down. But the Owl, glancing from
the heights of an avenue of elms, could see the long
shadow that rippled on the surface of the river,
and saw it turn easily and by-pass the Island, with
yards to spare.

Even Woo could see that it might have been
better if the log had hit the shore; even from this
height its speed was visible; and Woo had passed
the Stoat who had first started off to warn Potter and
his friends. The log would be there long before
Stoaty was anywhere near . . .

There was a rush of air through his wings as Owl
came diving like a feathered comet from the summer
spaces; and one or two folk who were digging on
the bank glanced up in alarm as they heard the faint
sound of his descent. With a bump he landed on the
warm green moss, and said quickly:

'Where's Potter?'

Mole-the-Miller pointed with a big pink paw.

'Under the water,' he said.

Woo glanced up-stream, half-expecting to see the
huge timber already bearing down on them through
the winding banks. But the water was innocent of
it as yet.

The Runaway Timber

'Listen, you folk,' he said urgently; and they stopped work immediately. 'There's a log, twenty feet long, floating down the river. It'll be here at any minute. Can we prepare to stop it?'

No-folk asked how a huge timber like that had happened to be careering down the river of a sudden; there was no time, if Owl said it would be here at any minute. Three Ferrets dived straight into the water, swimming strongly to the far bank, each with a rope end in his paws. Mole-the-Miller was with them, diving cleanly into the depths of the cool stream; for Potter must be warned. If he swam up to the surface when the log came past, he might easily bump his Ottery head on it—and it would be more than a gentle bump.

It so happened that old Potter had stopped digging his holes for the moment, and was swimming below-water, going up-stream, to look for some larger pebbles that might be used to brace the posts once they were in position. It was because of this change of position that of a sudden he became a fairly astonished folk; for when he rose to the surface to breathe some more Potter-breath, several strange occurrences were a-going on.

In the first place, a huge shadow, as long as a pine-tree, was drifting swiftly down-water as he made to surface. Well used to avoiding things in the stream, he swerved to one side and shot through the ripples into the sunshine—to see hordes of folk dashing madly up and down the banks, shouting for all they were worth, and hurling lengths of rope and such across the water. But even as Potter saw and heard this amazing disturbance, he felt himself dragged beneath the surface again by a very determined pair of paws wrapped round his heels.

It was Mole-the-Miller, thinking Potter was just about to bump his Ottery old head on various timbers and such that were about these days.

Potter grew annoyed. There was something highly interesting a-going on, and no-folk had told him a thing about it. So he struck out in the water, dragged this heavy form after him, broke into the sunshine, and saw it was Mole.

'Mole,' he began firmly, paddling on the ripples; but Mole interrupted him, panting hard through his whiskers—

'Potter, there's a log run amok, down-river!'

These words were enough for a river-folk. Now he knew what all the shouting was about, and all the rope-hurling, and the monstrous shadow that had passed overhead just now, and Moles pulling him down by the legs of such an unexpected sudden. Where the log had come from, and why it was drifting down-stream, he didn't know. But it *was*, so he must do something about it immediately.

Now Otter could swim pretty fast against the current. *With* the current you could scarcely see him shift, he was so quick. He was after that floating timber like a fish, splitting the water as his paws struck, struck, struck and pressed it behind his sleek body. Before he neared Stricken Oak, half-way between Otter's Island and Silver Falls, he saw the great shadow ahead of him; and he rose like an arrow, to break surface not a yard behind the mighty log.

Above him beat strong wings, as Woo Owl and a dozen other Birds caught up with the timber. The folk along the banks were being left slowly behind, for the current was deceptively swift for a summer's day.

Potter sized the situation up, and knew there was just a chance to save the timber before it was drawn over Silver Falls and lost to them for ever— because they would never be able to lift its weight from the canyon below.

'Woo!' he called, as he strove to push the end of the log to one side and steer it to strike the bank, 'can you and the other birds fetch ropes?'

Woo heard but faintly, though he understood. They wheeled, with a threshing of pinions in the sunlit air, and swooped down to where the Otters and Badgers and Squirrels and Stoats and Weasels and Rabbits were running and scampering and racing along the banks, already sure they had lost.

As the birds flew back, with long ropes trailing from their beaks, Potter struggled to swing the log, to make it hit the bank and become jammed; but its weight was too much; its speed was too great.

The ropes snaked down as the Otter shouted orders; and as their ends smacked the surface of the water he dived below the log and rose swiftly on the other side, while a bird swooped down and seized the end as Potter held it up.

Within three minutes, six ropes were drawn about the timber; but the roar of the Silver Falls was now plain in the distance. Before their voice rose and was deafening, another four ropes were drawn around the log; and now the birds beat their wings in frenzy, while Potter lashed the ripples with his onslaught. While the birds strove to break the speed of the timber by flying against it, Potter struggled to send it into the bank.

But the current was strengthening, second by second, as the water went surging over the brink of the Falls, to drop thunderously to the canyon below.

In the air, wings threshed, and ropes strained. In the water, the ripples were churned to fury. Along the banks came the Woodlanders, racing desperately to catch up and lend their strength before it was too late.

The Falls were nearer; their voice was clearer.

The timber drifted, swifter, swifter.

Time waited, and watched.

The race was on.

Chapter 13

The Bridge grows Day by Day

THE birds could do nothing save beat their wings against the tugging of the ropes, as the great timber raced onwards towards the roaring Falls. The folk who were pelting with all their breath along the banks could do nothing at all, for the race was lost to them. While they stumbled over tree-roots, darting between the trunks and swerving onto the next path beside the river, the log slipped smoothly and with a terrible inevitability towards the brink of water that plunged, a second later, to the abyss of the canyon.

Only Potter-the-Otter could make any difference to the onward surge of the timber; and he needed help. He was just about to give up hope of saving the log, and to make for the safety of calmer waters himself, when Woo Owl, flying overhead with a rope tugging in his talons, had such a stupendous idea that he hooted in surprise at his own cleverness.

But there was little time left—if any at all. Not twenty yards down-water there lay the brink of Silver Falls; and the speed of the log was rising

with every yard as it felt and obeyed the current's
quickening pull.

Woo Owl sized things up, and made his decision.

Two Jackdaws were pulling at ropes round the
front end of the log. Two Jays were pulling two
more, also at the front. At the rear, six ropes rose to
four Rooks and a pair of Ravens.

'Ahoy!' hooted Owl of a sudden, and dropped
his rope, circling the other birds with a mighty
swerve of his wings. 'Let go the ropes, you Jays and
you Jackdaws! *Let them drop!*'

They did, more in surprise than obedience. But
Woo was diving for the Rooks and Ravens, urging
them to hold on and to alter their straining course—

'Make this way, this way! Swing the ropes over,
this way!'

They veered, without hesitation. The ropes
swung, taut as bow-strings, until the birds were
beating fiercely at right-angles to the course of the
river. Woo Owl glanced below him, and a grunt of
satisfaction came from his chest, as he struggled to
complete his plan. Folding his wings tightly he went
into a steep dive, and spread them to arrest his
swoop within a few feet of Potter-the-Otter, still
striking out in the water.

'Swing the log over at the stern!' called Woo,
'swing into the right fork of the river!'

Potter said nothing. He had no time to look up
to see what the birds were doing. He had been

struggling for many long minutes, trying to do just what Owl was telling him to do now, but without success. Yet Owl was a wise old folk. Potter tried even harder, and, as his paws pushed at the end of the timber while his feet struck out behind him, he was amazed; for the great log swung, slowly but with gathering speed.

Woo Owl gasped in relief. His plan was working. At the Silver Falls, the river forked, and one waterway veered to the east, finally to join the stream that flowed at the bottom of Sweethallow Valley. Now, as the Rooks and Ravens flew towards one bank of the river, their ropes tugged the stern of the log that way. Potter, pushing in the same direction, was making good progress; and slowly the mighty piece of timber was swinging sideways at the rear end, while the front, released from the ropes of the Jays and Jackdaws, swung the opposite way, and now pointed towards the branch of the stream.

The Woodlanders along the banks pulled up, panting their little furry hearts out. They could see now that there was nothing they could do, and no point in their running further. But they saw also that the log was definitely swinging away from the falls, and nosing for the branch to the east.

In less than a minute it was all over. The Rooks and Ravens, beating strongly, kept the stern of the log well turned; and Potter helped them in the water.

The Bridge grows Day by Day

Even now he was clinging to the timber itself, to ride with it into the safety of the branch-stream— whereas a few minutes ago he had been ready to abandon the log and leave it to the brink of the hungry waters of the Falls. Now he clambered on board, and stood upright for a moment, wobbling violently but waving his paws in high delight.

With a mighty swoop, Woo Owl swerved past his head, and called out: 'Good work, Potter!'

'Good work yourself!' called he, for he knew the idea had been Owl's. He didn't know whether his feathery old friend had heard the reply, because at the moment he was having to keep his feet as the great log rolled beneath him. Before he had succeeded, it had swerved finally under the tugging of the birds, and the front end drove into the bank, which jutted slightly into the stream.

Potter gave a hoot of alarm, shot forward off his balance, and vanished in a shower of spray. The log swung ponderously, until the rear end struck the opposite bank, and the length of it became wedged across the stream.

A cheer rose from the fur-folk who were coming along the pathways; it was echoed by the birds as they dived low, releasing the last of the ropes and hovering above the swimming Otter to see he was unhurt by his headlong tumble. But he was in fine fettle, and climbed back on to the log to give a war-dance for his large audience.

The Bridge grows Day by Day

The log was saved. It would take much work to salvage it from the river; but it would be worth it. One tree less would have to be felled in Shingle Spinney, if this were brought back and used for the bridge.

It was a full day's work. Mr. Nibble and Old Stripe made haste to build a second barrow, and Scruff Fox, remembering an old gardening-cart he had lying in the summer-house, went along and fetched it back with him. When the runaway timber had been rolled back to the spot where the bridge would be built, the other logs were wheeled down the woodland pathways on the three barrows; and where the bends in the path were too sharp, well then, they made new tracks between the nearby trees.

In three days, Potter and Mole-the-Miller had finished the sinking of the holes that would receive the twelve upright posts. Then the problem of raising them and burying their bases had to be dealt with.

'Only one thing to do,' said Skip Squirrel; and he pointed upwards to where the oak-trees covered the sky above the river with their spreading boughs.

'And what's that?' asked Mole, who was a folk used rather to digging and tunnelling in the earth than climbing trees.

Skip waved a confident paw.

'We just sling a rope over those boughs, bring the other end down again, and use them for cranes!'

The Bridge grows Day by Day

'Well well,' nodded Old Stripe admiringly.

'Excellent!' boomed Woo, and flew straight up to the lowest branch, there to jump up and down with portly vigour. 'Strong as we could wish!' he called down.

They made their plans. Skimble the Gnome and ten of his fellows climbed the trunks of the overhanging trees, and stood-by along the boughs, to

place the ropes and keep them in position. One by one the birds flew upwards, trailing the cords behind them, to fly over the boughs and down again, leaving a Goblin to place each one securely. From below, Potter-the-Otter sighted the positions of his holes in the stream-bed, gave the position to Scruff Fox, who waved his paw to the Gnomes, according to which way Potter told him.

The Bridge grows Day by Day

As the timbers were sunk into the river, by the weight of rocks slung to the ends, the two longer ones were rolled across the water. One end was held firmly on the west bank, and the other end secured to Potter's blue boat 'Bunty,' which carried it in an arc across the ripples to the far bank, where it was lifted out.

The Woodlanders worked as a great team, and the Goblins laboured almost harder than they. Day by day, week by week, the timber was placed, fitted, braced and secured. The trees were loud with sounds —the sawing of wood as the posts and beams were cut to their required length; the hammering of mallets as Mr. Nibble and several others drove in the stout wooden pegs.

A thousand holes were drilled; and a thousand pegs cut to fit them. Two hundred planks were made, and smoothed, and shaped, and fitted one to its neighbour. All day, while the sunshine lit the busy scene, fifty Woodlanders toiled, and twenty Gnomes. More than often, folk would come up from the Valley, bringing tools and timber, to help with the bridge that would one day carry their barrows to the Wood, laden with peat and with pine-cones, fir and sweet cedar logs.

The River knew the raising of this second bridge along its friendly banks. No beam was built upon the waters before they were whirling and dancing around in surprise. And when the folk went slowly homeward after a long day's toil, the water lapped and chuckled beneath the silent stars, slapping and swirling round the posts and ringing them with ripples of silver the night long.

Potter-the-Otter, sitting one evening on his Island, drinking a pot of sweet ale with his good friend the Badger, looked down-water and said:

'You know something, Old Stripe?'

'Very little,' said Old Stripe, for he was an honest folk.

'I shall see the bridge from here. When the lanterns are lit along it by night.'

'Ah,' said the Badger, and felt an inner twinge of envy; for no lamplit bridge was visible from Badger's Beech, or ever would be unless the river made up its watery old mind and altered course for the heart of the Wood.

'So I hope you'll come along for a pipe and a sup of ale,' went on Potter, who was a hospitable folk, as were most of the Woodlanders. 'Then we can sit here and look at the lights on Goblin Bridge.'

'Ah,' nodded Old Stripe again, while he thought all this out for himself. Then he said, 'I'd very much like to do that, Potter-the-Otter. Come to think of it,' he added, because he'd just this minute come to think of it, 'I've always come along here for a pipe and a sup, even when there hasn't been a Bridge to look at. Except of course when you don't happen to be in.'

'And when I don't happen to be that,' nodded his Ottery friend, 'it means I'm probably at Badger's Beech, a-doing of much the same delightful kind of thing.'

Old Stripe nodded again; then a slight frown returned to his stripey brows. For there was something old Potter had just said that lingered in his mind. What was it now? Something about the bridge, yes. Something about—

'Potter,' he said, as he remembered what it was, 'why did you call it the *Goblin* Bridge, just now?'

'Did I?' asked he. 'Well I never.'

'Well, why did you?' persisted Stripe.

'I don't know,' said his friend. 'Except that it seems a fitting sort of name, I suppose. It only seems a few weeks ago when the Hobgoblins first came to Deep Wood, and here we are in the middle of building a bridge.'

'It *is* only a few weeks ago,' nodded Stripe, as he watched the smoke from his pipe against the sundown over the trees. 'And in a way the Goblins were responsible for the whole idea.'

'It was your idea, Old Stripey,' Potter reminded him.

'Well I *thought* of it, yes; but you see I was thinking of what young Skimble the Gnome had said: he and his folk wanted work to do. And you ferried Tufty Squirrel across the river at the very same time, and I heard about that, too. So it sort of—well—

connected. Folks wanting work to do and folks having to be ferried. It all kind of—well—fitted in.'

'There you are, then,' nodded Potter. 'What do you think of it, then?'

'Of what?'

'The name. Goblin Bridge.'

'Goblin Bridge,' said Stripe, rolling the name round his considering old tongue. And by this time the two of them had said it so often that there was already a friendly and familiar sound to it. 'Yes,' declared Stripe, 'I like it.'

'Good,' said the Otter. 'Then we'll tell them, first thing in the morning.'

'And see if they like it too,' nodded his friend.

They sat for a moment more, watching the starlight as it gleamed among the ripples' furrowed wake. In the mind of Potter he could already see the lanterns, strung along the graceful bridge, and their reflection in the same ripples as he was watching now. The night air was still as a breath held; no leaf moved; no sound was there but the river's lulling moods.

'Old Stripe,' murmured Potter-the-Otter, softly.

The river murmured with him. There was no reply.

Old Stripe was fast asleep, with his pot of ale tilted on his furry old knee, and his briar pipe resting on his furry old chin. Maybe he dreamed of a bridge across the Wild River, as he had dreamed before, once in a sunbeam.

Chapter 14

Goblin Bridge

AUTUMN was coming to Deep Wood. In Badger's Beech a breeze whispered it down a chimney—'Autumn—can you hear it?' From Owl's house in the great tree there fell a shower of leaves, brown and gold and yellow; and their tiny rustle whispered—'Autumn—do you see it?' And as Potter-the-Otter opened his front door to row down the river to where the new bridge spanned the ripples, the cold air pinched his nose and said: 'Autumn—do you feel it?'

Potter-the-Otter did. But there was no time to go thinking about it this morning. For many weeks the folk of the Wood and of the Valley had toiled on their bridge-building, together with the twenty Hobgoblins. Now it was almost completed. From the west bank to the east there rose the great timbers in a gracious curve; and the waters of the river lapped merrily around the sturdy posts beneath.

The Woodlanders worked on, putting the finishing touches to their building; a beam was being strengthened near the middle, for the wood was knotty; a plank was being shifted, for there was a narrow crack; one of the lantern-posts was being straightened, for it was of gnarled and obstinate walnut. The Goblins were helping, as always, but most of the Sweethallow folk were down in their homeland valley. It was almost autumn, and they must dig peat and cut it into blocks; they must gather fircones and pinecones; and pine-needles and cedar logs. Much of this would go to Deep Wood for the hearths and the thatching in the spring of the next year.

Skip Squirrel, as he perched precariously atop the tallest lamp-post at one end of Goblin Bridge, was talking to Skimble the Gnome, as they polished the lantern's glass with vigorous hands and paws. Skimble was whistling a ditty, on and off, for he was the happiest folk in the land.

'I never knew there was so much fun to be had, Skip Squirrel,' he said, breaking off his tune, 'in *not* making mischief.'

'In not making it?' said Skip, looking at his reflection in the lamp-glass and thinking it mighty fine.

Skimble nodded, looking at his grand white beard in the other side of the lantern.

'We thought we were having fun, all right, when we went around snuffing a folk's candle or souring his milk.'

Goblin Bridge

Skip Squirrel didn't say nuffin; because *he* knew all about folk's milk being sour.

'But this is a far finer way of doing things!' went on the Goblin, and tugged his beard to see if the Goblin in the lamp-glass tugged it too. He did, and he nodded in satisfaction. 'If ever we get our magic powers back,' he said quietly, 'we'll use them to do good, instead of mischief.'

'Well,' said Skip thoughtfully, 'there's a deal of good to be done in the world, so I've heard.'

Skimble polished his last glass and nodded vigorously.

'Then we shall do it,' he said solemnly.

As he said that, he felt a queer, tingly feeling come over him. It began in his toes, deep inside his golden-buckled shoes, and flowed all over him until it tickled the top of his head, underneath his moss-green hat.

'That's funny,' he said.

'What is?' asked Skip, who hadn't felt anything at all.

'I don't know. But it's gone now.'

'What a pity,' said the Squirrel, who wasn't really listening, for he was eager to get on with the next lamp along the bridge.

He scampered down the tall lantern-posts and up the other, leaving Skimble to wonder for a moment about the queer feeling he'd had when he'd been talking about doing good in the world.

Goblin Bridge

Old Stripe was painting a piece of carving, at the base of Skip's lamp, where somefolk had overlooked it. The rest of the bridge had been painted a deep green; the lantern-posts were brown; and the lanterns a shining black.

'Scruff Fox,' he said as he plied his careful brush, 'you know something?'

'A little more, every day,' said Scruff deedily as he watched, 'but it's slow going.'

'What I mean,' said Stripe, 'is that it won't be so very long before Candles the Hedgehog comes here for the autumn.'

'With special candles,' nodded his friend, 'for the biggest lamps in the Woodland!'

'With special ones,' nodded Stripe, 'exactly.' And his small pink tongue crept out as his brush went up, and crept back as it came down. He wasn't thirsty but just concentrating.

'Woo Owl has been flying down over Dingle Copse, these last few days,' Scruff told him, 'to see if Hedgehog is on his way. Any day now.'

'Any day now,' nodded Stripe, as his tongue sidled out for another peep at the paint-brush. Any day now, there would be much happening. Old Candles would come, for one thing; and the Valley folk would be bringing their stores across to the Wood—maybe across the new bridge, as it was nearly finished; and the Woodlanders would be loading up the same barrows for taking back, laden with all manner of winter cheer.

Autumn was almost the busiest season of the year—and this time there had been a new bridge built, for good measure.

It had created much comment, for miles around. Folk had come to look at it, from Tall Timberland, Mole Meadow, and Briar Hill. Birds, flying high above the Wood, had glanced down and seen the strange structure for the first time, And the word had gone round: 'There's a bridge going up, across the Wild River!'

There was only one folk who had yet to see it for himself, and Woo Owl was out looking for him every morning. Soon the little traveller, Candles the Hedgehog, must come; and Owl made it his first business, immediately after breakfast. Sometimes Candles would enter the Wood by way of Dingle Copse; sometimes from Sweethallow; sometimes they never saw his coming at all, but suddenly found him at the steps of the Badger's house, knocking on the door.

It was six days after Owl had first begun his daily search when the candle-seller was glimpsed, far across the trees to the south, where Heather Hill rose as a rampart to the Wood.

Woo wheeled in his flight and dived low over Goblin Bridge, where folk were gathered in the morning sunshine. They were startled by his voice as he cried down to them—

'Candles is coming! Hedgehog is here!' And he was off again, to greet the little traveller, many miles distant. For Owl it was an easy journey and a swift one; but the prickle-folk had half a day's march before him yet.

'Candles, at last,' said Old Stripe happily, 'and the bridge is finished!'

'He can be the first traveller to cross it into the Wood!' cried Skip Squirrel; and the Badger looked at him, his eyes bright.

'Now that's a friendly thought, young Skip!' he said, and wandered off to see a Jackdaw. The bird nodded and talked with him, then spread his black and shining wings, rising to follow the course Woo was making through the sunlit air. Hedgehog would be led round through the Valley, so he could reach the border of the Wood at the edge of Wild River, where now there stood Goblin Bridge.

By noon, the traveller was within two miles of the Valley; and by tea-time half-way up the West slopes. Many of the Sweethallow folk were with him now, helping him with his barrow; and some of them had barrows of their own, for the first of the stores were being taken up to the Wood.

The candle-seller had heard from Woo Owl about the bridge being finished; and though he was surprised, there came a twinkle deep in his eyes as he said:

'Of course it's finished—I told you I wanted to

see it when I came in the Autumn. Besides,' he added, 'I've been helping to build it, in a way.'

Woo looked at the barrow, and saw that it looked a little fatter than usual, under its gay canvas cover.

'You've brought them?' he whispered eagerly.

Hedgehog nodded. 'I have,' he said, 'just as I promised.'

Woo spread his wings and was away, rising over the slopes to where the Wild River ran.

'Open the lanterns!' he called, as he landed with an excited thump on the planking. 'Hedgehog has brought the candles!'

There were few folk on the bridge, for those who could walk any distance had gone to meet the traveller, long ago. But the lamps were opened, one by one, and left ready to receive the large candles that were made for them in a secret cave on the other side of the world.

By evening, Hedgehog the Traveller stood beneath the last of the cedar trees at the Valley's western brink, and looked across the toadstools to see Goblin Bridge, spanning the Wild River before his very eyes.

It was beautiful, and just as he had imagined it in his thoughts, while his feet had trod the pathways of the world. A bridge that stood fine and strong across the tumbling waters; that had the strength and the grace of any tree in the Wood; for the trees had made it and were part of it.

Goblin Bridge

Something deep down in the prickle-folk's heart was trying to bring a tear to his eyes; for the bridge was as lovely as a living tree. He knew, without having been here at the building, how many hours of toil were in those majestic beams; how many timbers had been felled and drawn and shaped and cut and hammered and fitted and braced and finally painted; how many small paws had gone to the raising of this graceful thing.

But Hedgehog cared little to show his feelings too clearly. There was a gruff grumble from him as he swallowed something in his throat.

'Well now,' he said simply, and his words scarcely faltered, 'I've seen some bridges in me time, the world over, but never a one as fine as this.' He blinked quickly, and gave a decided sniff. 'No,' he said softly, 'never.'

'I'm glad you think it's a fair bridge,' murmured Old Stripe quietly, for he knew what was passing through the little folk's thoughts.

'And you'll be the first folk to cross it!' said Skip Squirrel—for it had been his idea, and he was secretly proud of it.

'I shall?' said Hedgehog, and his eyes grew bright.

'Well then,' he said, and there was a catch in his small prickly voice, 'well then, let's—let's be going!'

They stood back from his little barrow, and let him take the handles in his paws. And only Old Stripe saw how they trembled with happiness.

At least a dozen Valley-dwellers were ready with their own barrows; but they waited, now. Though no-folk had said so, they knew this was rather a special moment.

There was a stillness in the air that comes to autumn as a lull before the winds. Beyond the trees there swam the homeward sun, shedding his crimson beams among the leafy heights and dappling the moss with limpid pools of light. A single star was poised, a million miles away in the great circle of the skies, and a cloud sat, fat and sun-pink, above a pine-tree's distant crown.

The sun, the star, and the fat pink cloud seemed to hold their breath in heaven as Hedgehog the Traveller, who was come to the Wood by Autumn, started off with his barrow of candles, to trundle it over the brown and friendly pathway until the wheels met the bridge, and trundled with a new and louder sound, as though they were surprised to find stout planking where once was a rippling stream.

Behind Hedgehog there moved the folk from Sweethallow, wheeling their barrows laden with good store for their friends of Deep Wood.

From the great blue space of the twilight-sky, the single star looked down. The plump, pink cloud was still, as the winds of the South held their breath.

The sun was sinking beyond Briar Hill, when the first traveller crossed Goblin Bridge.

The timbers were loud with the wheels of his

barrow and of the Valley folk's loaded stores. Old
Stripe stepped with a spring in his sprightly old
feet, and Skip Squirrel danced beside him. Scruff
there came and Potter, and Mole-the-Miller too;
and above and between the lanterns flew Woo Owl,
wing to wing with the Ravens and the Rooks, the
Jays and the Jackdaws, swooping and circling
above the jostling throng who crossed from the
land of the Valley to that of the Wood, carrying
cheer for Christmas tables and winter hearths.

* * *

A feast was held, that Autumn night; but before it
was joined there was a small ceremony by the
river's edge. Sixteen candles, each of them as fat as a
willow-bough, were fitted into the lamps across
Goblin Bridge; and Skimble the Gnome, with a
lighted taper in his hand, went from one to the
next, to touch the new white wick. The flames took
and stood as silver crocuses, to shine at last across
the bridge, to wink and shimmer down upon the
rippling water of the stream, to gleam among the
shadows of the trees.

Old Stripe stood watching, next to Hedgehog the
Traveller, from beneath a friendly oak. His paw
strayed, and gripped the candle-seller's.

'It's as though a chain of stars were strung across
the river . . . ' he murmured happily.

Goblin Bridge

'Linking your land with the Valley,' nodded Hedgehog.

And Mole-the-Miller, who was a sentimental old folk beneath his smart black velvety waistcoat, nodded silently, and one small tear fell—as one quite often did when he felt even more happy than always —from one small bright eye, and glistened in the lights of Goblin Bridge.

Skimble the Gnome came down from the last lamp, and stood himself on the moss. There was a strange feeling over him, spread from his toes to his head. It was the same feeling he had felt not long ago, when he'd been talking to Skip Squirrel. But now, as he felt it tingling all over him, he was no longer wondering what it could be. He knew. And he knew his fellows were feeling it too.

He said nothing of it to any except his own friends. Later, they agreed, they would tell the Woodlanders.

It was when the feast was waxing towards the early hours of the next morning that Skimble went over to Old Stripe, the host of Badger's Beech.

For many hours, through the stilly autumn night, the merry-making had been loud and delightsome. The tables in the banqueting-hall were heaped with goodly things; and ruby ale and honey-wine had winked in goblets and ancient pots. Many a tune had been fiddled and piped and danced, while shadows jigged the ditty on the walls. But now, when folk were talking more quietly over a pot of wine and a pipe of baccy, Skimble the Goblin went to his host the Badger.

'We—we are leaving you,' was all he said; and said it softly.

'Leaving us?' said Stripe, his eyes wide with surprise.

'You see,' the Gnome explained, 'our magic powers have come back to us—we have felt it tingling through us, all the day.'

Old Stripe nodded slowly, not understanding, but happy for the Gnomes. Skip Squirrel had told him how Skimble had talked of having fun by doing good; and the Badger had thought it as fine a thing as ever he'd heard, for—as the Squirrel himself had said—there was much good ready for the doing in the world.

'So you must leave the Wood,' said Stripe slowly, and gave a sigh. 'Well, we shall miss you. Remember there's a place to come back to, if the mood moves you.'

'We shall, Old Stripe,' said Skimble, and bowed his puckish head. 'And we shall always remember, too, your kindness, and the kindness of your friends. We came to the Wood to make mischief, and you showed us a different way.'

Old Stripe said nothing about that. If the Hobgoblins had gained good from the trees here, they would take it away with them wherever they went; but it would still remain.

The Badger silenced the guests, later, and told them of the Goblins' new magic that had returned to them. A toast was drunk to the clink of tankards and the murmur of farewell. A song was sung, and a word was said, and the goblins bowed low to the great company, just as they had bowed in the light of lavender-flames one long-ago night in Owl's Glade.

* * *

Dawn was still an hour distant when the Woodlanders and the Sweethallow Folk gathered outside Badger's Beech, to watch the going of the Goblins and to wave goodbye. The twenty small creatures formed a circle around the beech, and stood with their small buckled shoes together, and straightened their small green hats upon their heads. Then, as Skimble looked around him, and nodded happily, a strange thing happened.

It was as though each Gnome were touched of a sudden by blue fire; and for a moment the Woodlanders held their breath. The blue fire burned, and became a sapphire flame; and there ringed the tree those same-and-twenty lamps that once had wreathed between the spinneys, as Will-o'-the-Wisps above a darkling fen.

They rose into the silent air and circled, thrice, above the blue-lit moss, and drifted now as though a chain of jewels were strung about the glades.

Goblin Bridge

In the stillness was now that strange elfin laughter that had been heard in the Wood; but now there was joy in it, and no mischief more.

While Old Stripe and Hedgehog the Traveller stood before Badger's Beech, their friends and neighbours about them, the Gnomes went their blue-gleaming way among the glades, away and away until they met the Wild River's western bank, where the lanterns of the bridge burned bright.

Mole-the-Miller, standing beside little Skip Squirrel, felt a catch in his velvety breath as he heard himself saying:

'Good-bye, Skimble, good luck.'

The string of blue and drifting lights merged with the candles of the lamps as the Goblins crossed Goblin Bridge, to vanish, one by one, beyond the distant trees, where slept the Valley of Sweethallow in the night.